BEAN

ZOO PATROL SQUAD

MEDIEVAL MAYHEM

PENGUIN WORKSHOP

For Julie
—BB

ABOUT THE CREATOR

Brett Bean is an author, illustrator, and designer whose work has been featured across film, TV, comics, children's books, and more. He has lots of artwork and designs on his website, brettbean.com. He works from Los Angeles.

To learn more about the Zoo Patrol Squad, go to zoopatrolsquad.com.

PENGUIN WORKSHOP
An imprint of Penguin Random House LLC, New York

First published in the United States of America by Penguin Workshop,
an imprint of Penguin Random House LLC, New York, 2022

Visit us online at penguinrandomhouse.com.

Library of Congress Control Number: 2021043123

Manufactured in China

ISBN 9780593383384   10 9 8 7 6 5 4 3 2 1 HH

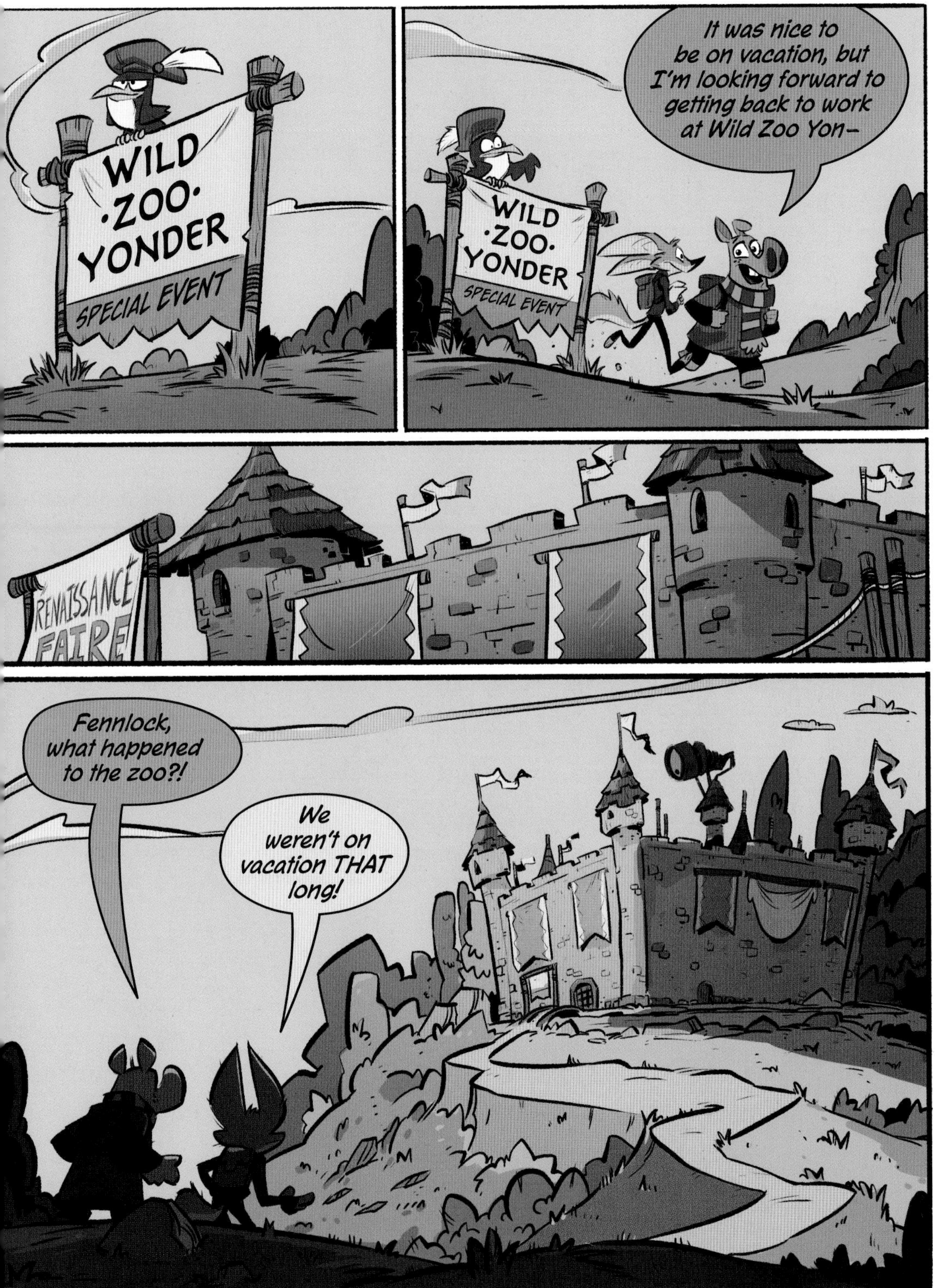

WILD ·ZOO· YONDER
SPECIAL EVENT
It was nice to be on vacation, but I'm looking forward to getting back to work at Wild Zoo Yon—
WILD ·ZOO· YONDER
SPECIAL EVENT
RENAISSANCE FAIRE
Fennlock, what happened to the zoo?!
We weren't on vacation THAT long!

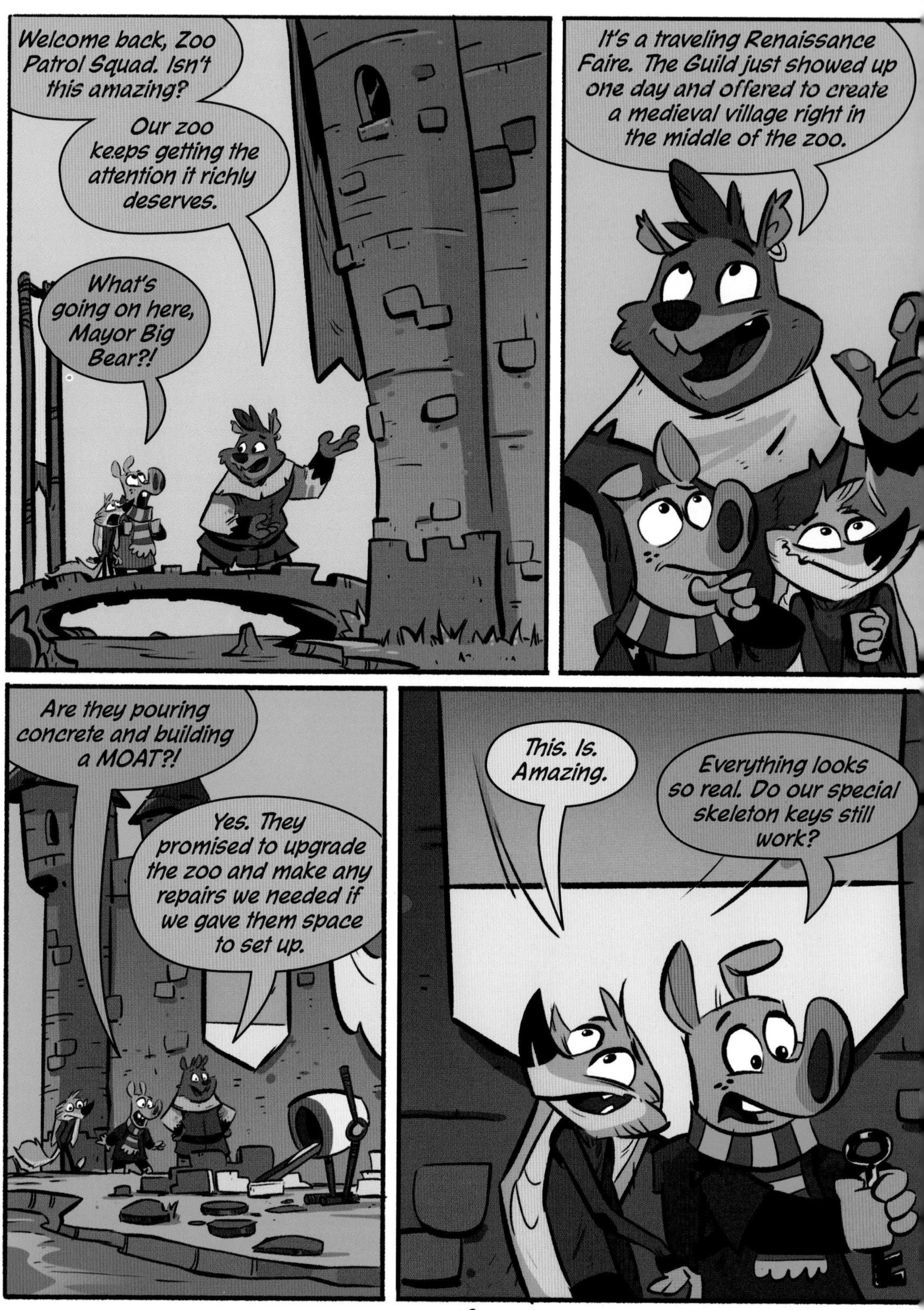
Welcome back, Zoo Patrol Squad. Isn't this amazing?
Our zoo keeps getting the attention it richly deserves.
What's going on here, Mayor Big Bear?!
It's a traveling Renaissance Faire. The Guild just showed up one day and offered to create a medieval village right in the middle of the zoo.
Are they pouring concrete and building a MOAT?!
Yes. They promised to upgrade the zoo and make any repairs we needed if we gave them space to set up.
This. Is. Amazing.
Everything looks so real. Do our special skeleton keys still work?

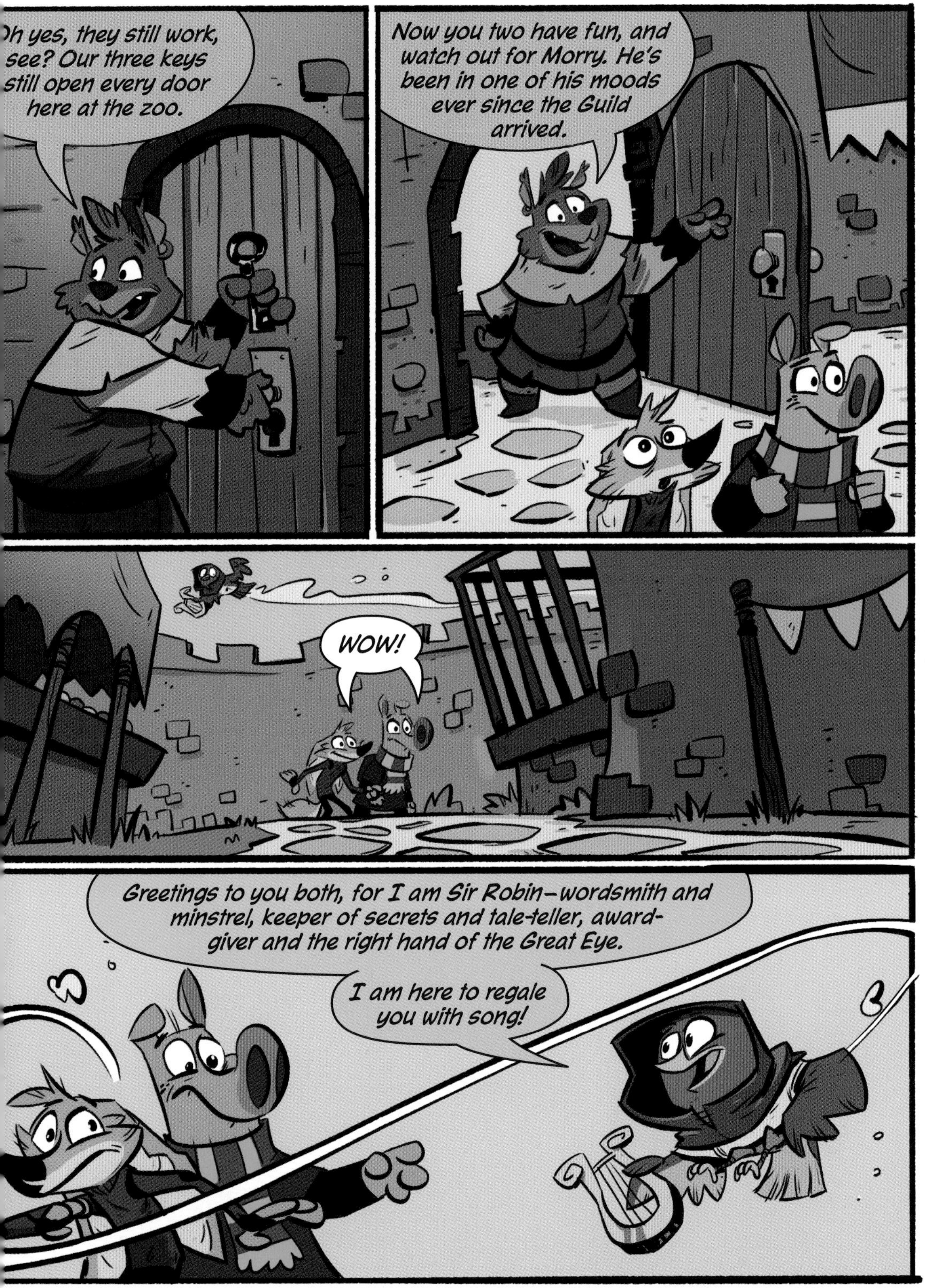
Oh yes, they still work, see? Our three keys still open every door here at the zoo.
Now you two have fun, and watch out for Morry. He's been in one of his moods ever since the Guild arrived.
WOW!
Greetings to you both, for I am Sir Robin—wordsmith and minstrel, keeper of secrets and tale-teller, award-giver and the right hand of the Great Eye.
I am here to regale you with song!

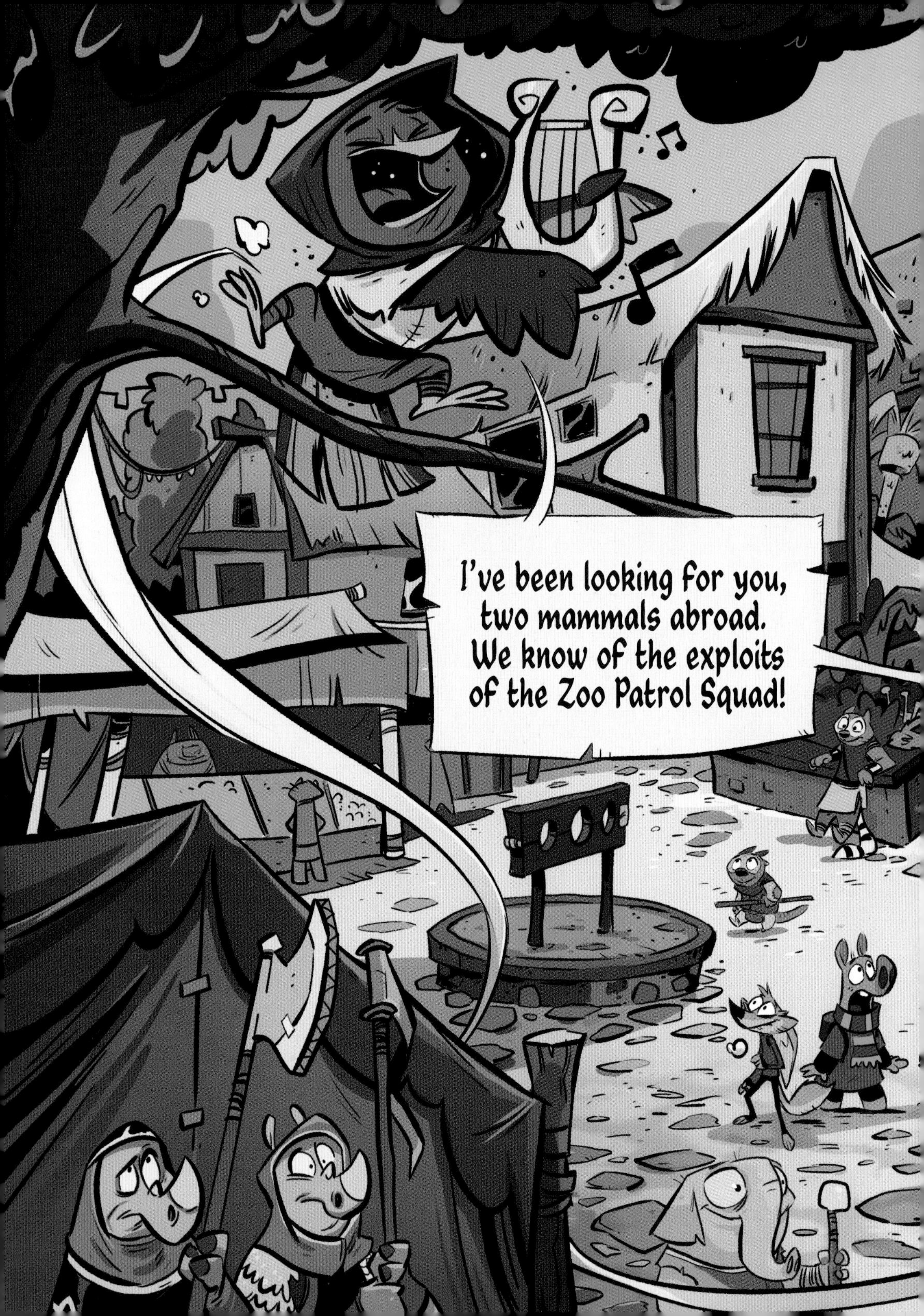
I've been looking for you, two mammals abroad. We know of the exploits of the Zoo Patrol Squad!

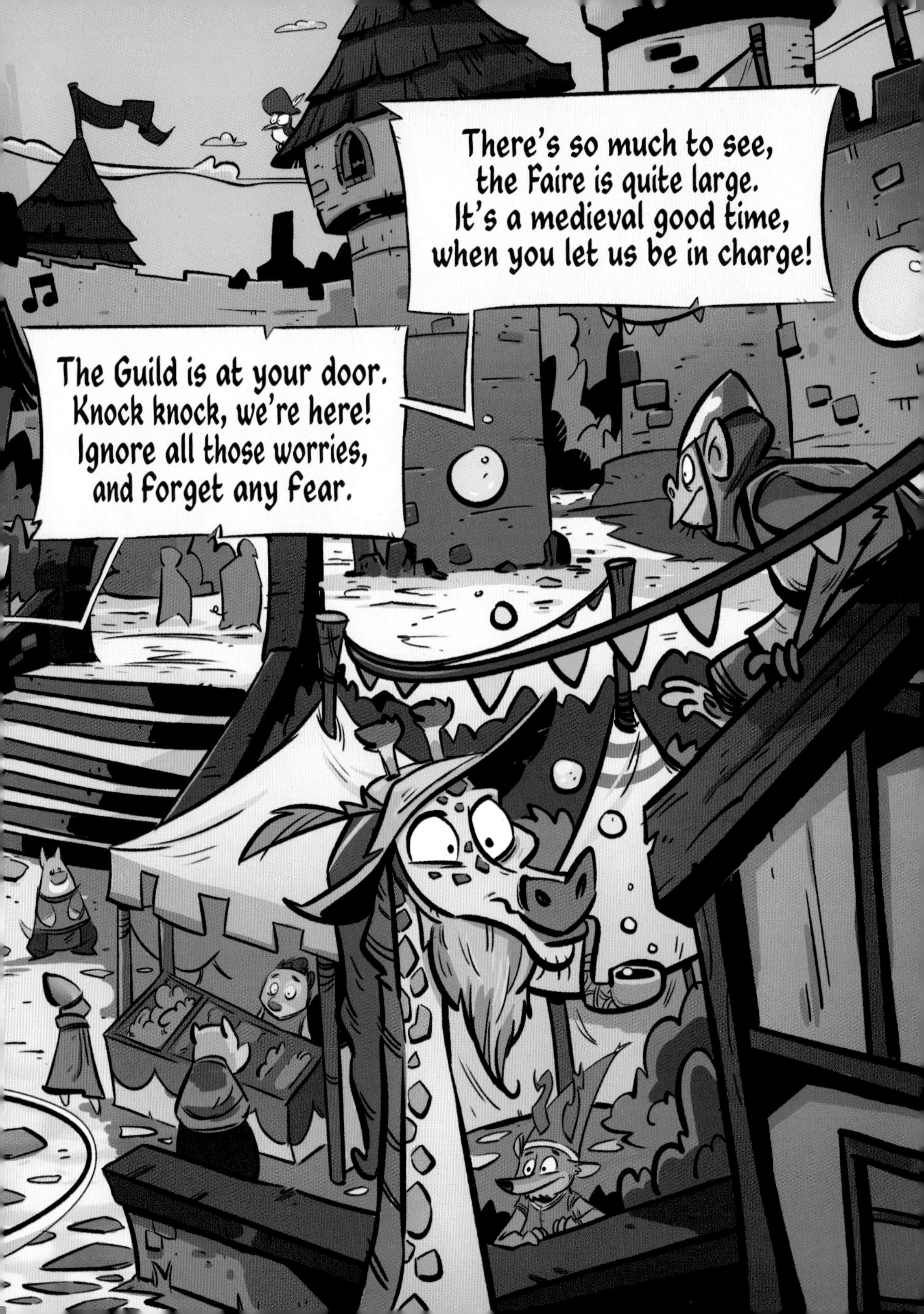

There's so much to see, the Faire is quite large. It's a medieval good time, when you let us be in charge!
The Guild is at your door. Knock knock, we're here! Ignore all those worries, and forget any fear.

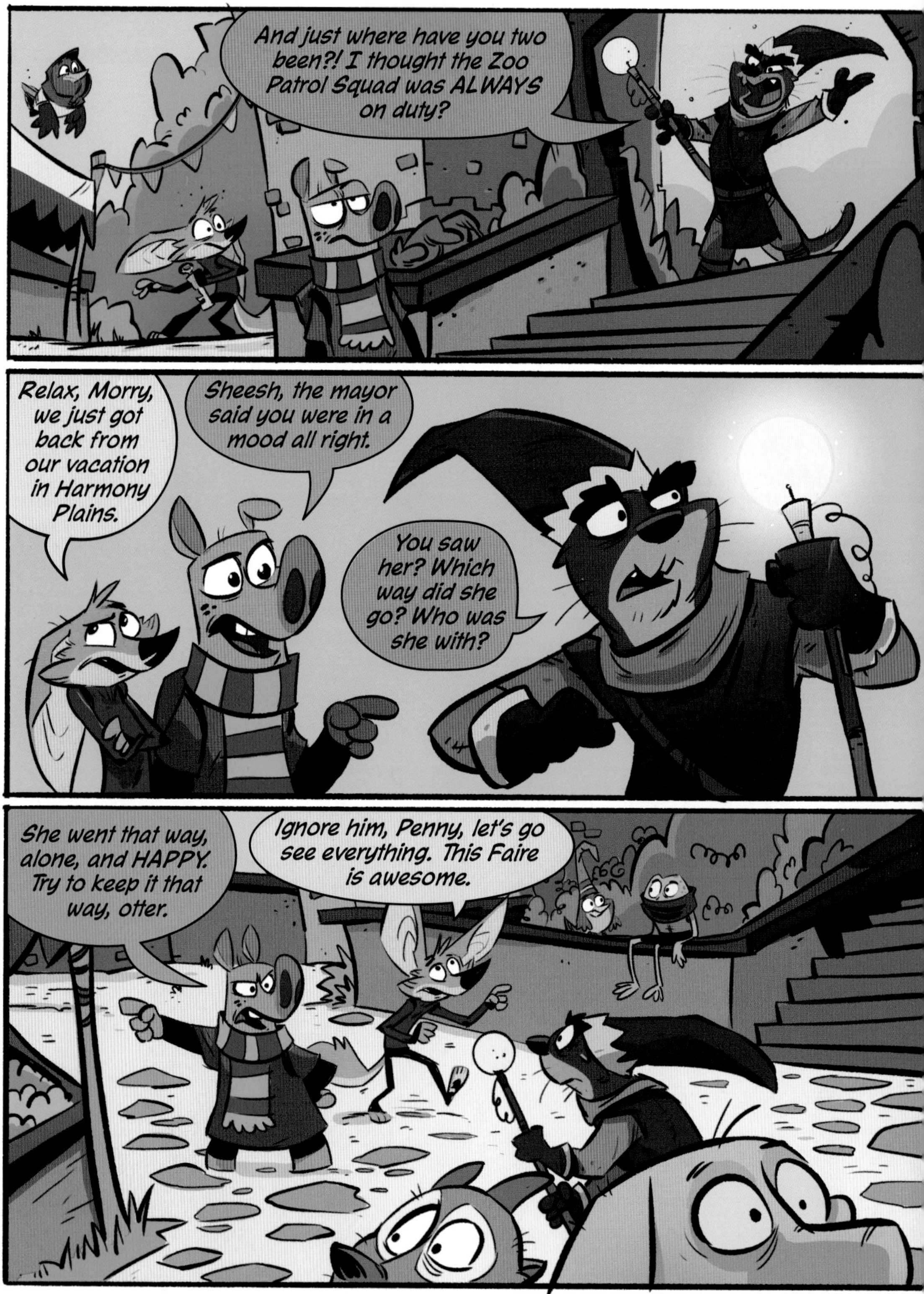
And just where have you two been?! I thought the Zoo Patrol Squad was ALWAYS on duty?
Relax, Morry, we just got back from our vacation in Harmony Plains.
Sheesh, the mayor said you were in a mood all right.
You saw her? Which way did she go? Who was she with?
She went that way, alone, and HAPPY. Try to keep it that way, otter.
Ignore him, Penny, let's go see everything. This Faire is awesome.

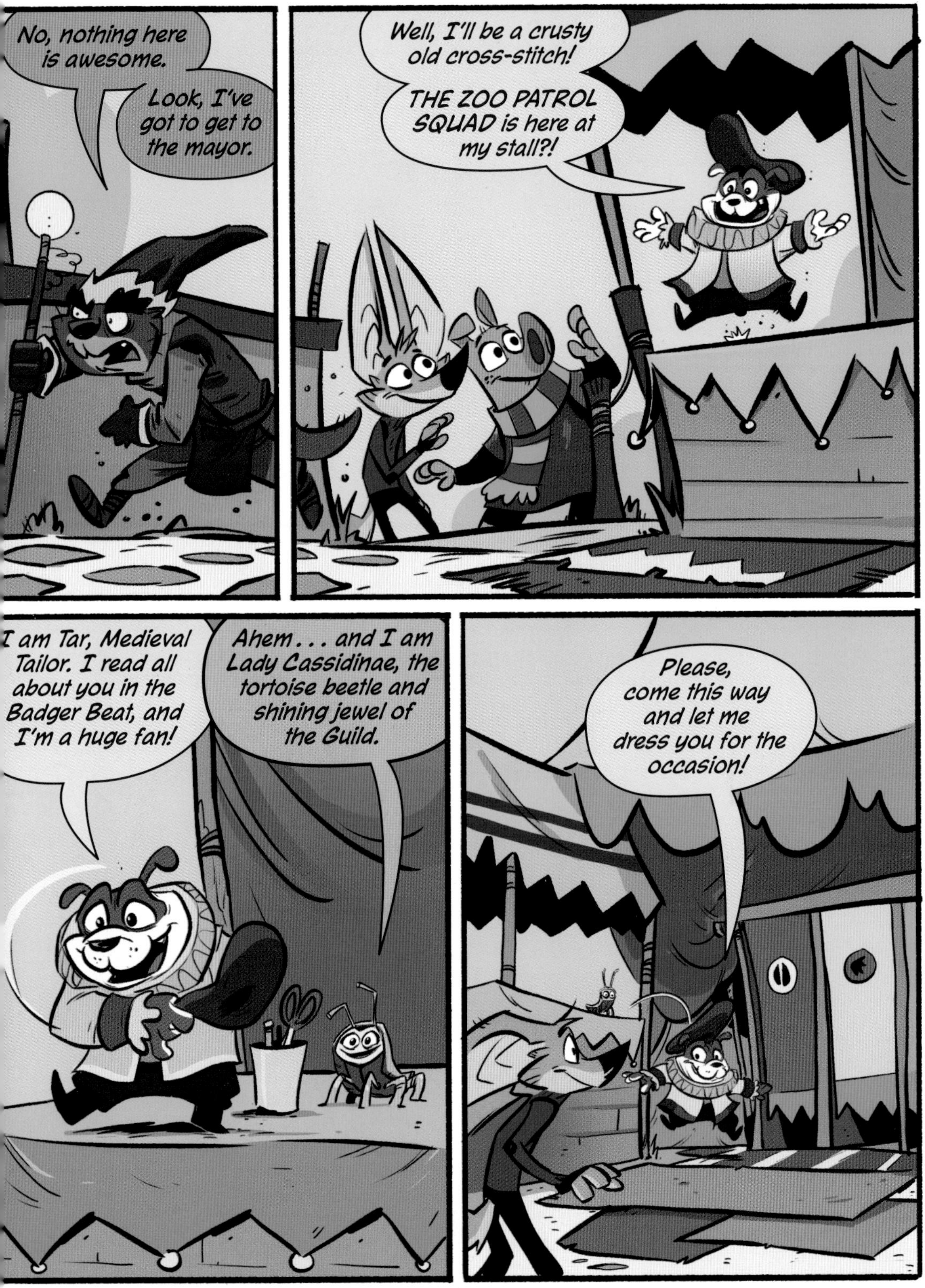

No, nothing here is awesome.
Look, I've got to get to the mayor.
Well, I'll be a crusty old cross-stitch!
THE ZOO PATROL SQUAD is here at my stall?!
I am Tar, Medieval Tailor. I read all about you in the Badger Beat, and I'm a huge fan!
Ahem . . . and I am Lady Cassidinae, the tortoise beetle and shining jewel of the Guild.
Please, come this way and let me dress you for the occasion!

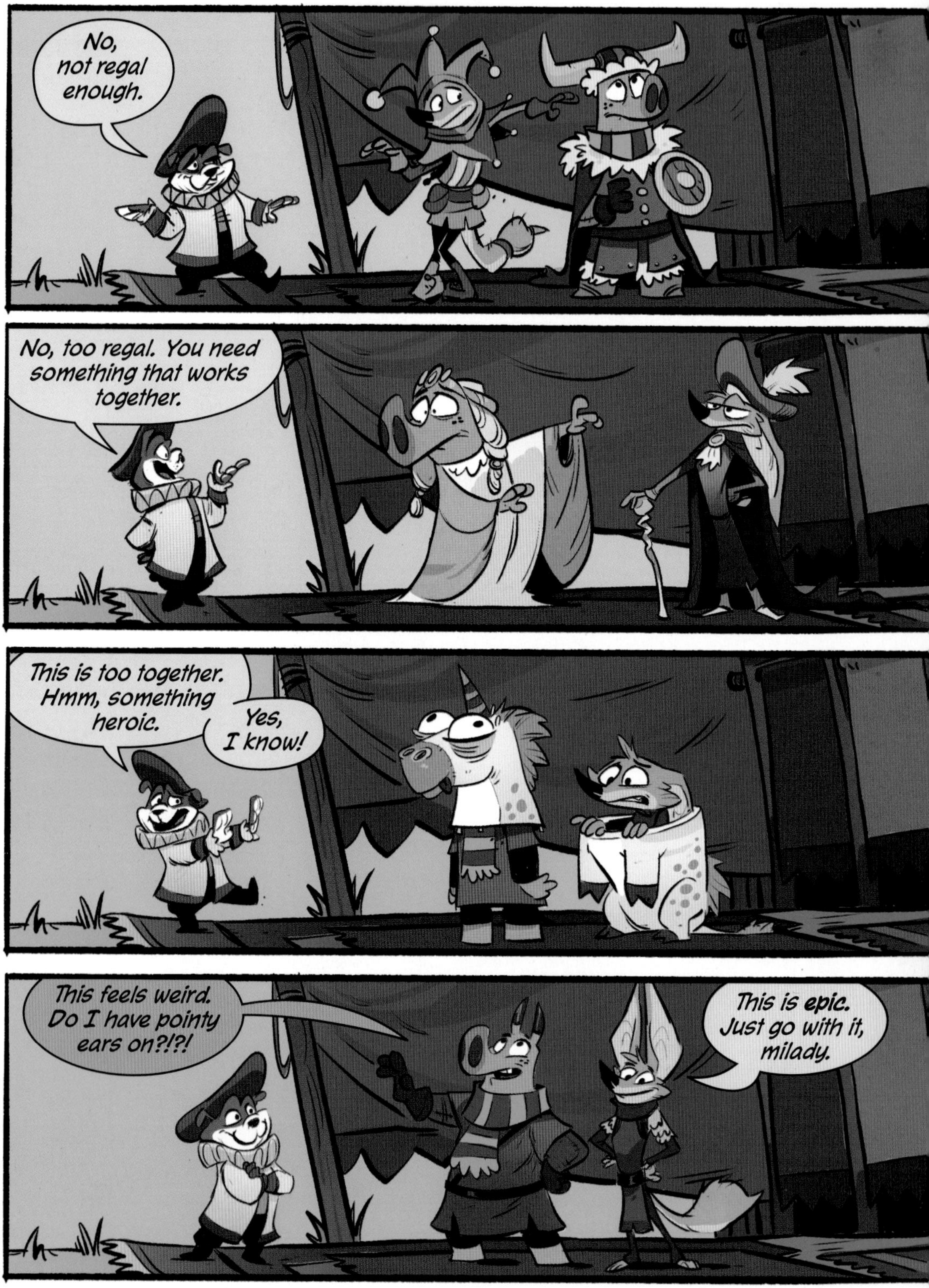
No, not regal enough.
No, too regal. You need something that works together.
This is too together. Hmm, something heroic.
Yes, I know!
This feels weird. Do I have pointy ears on?!?!
This is **epic.** Just go with it, milady.

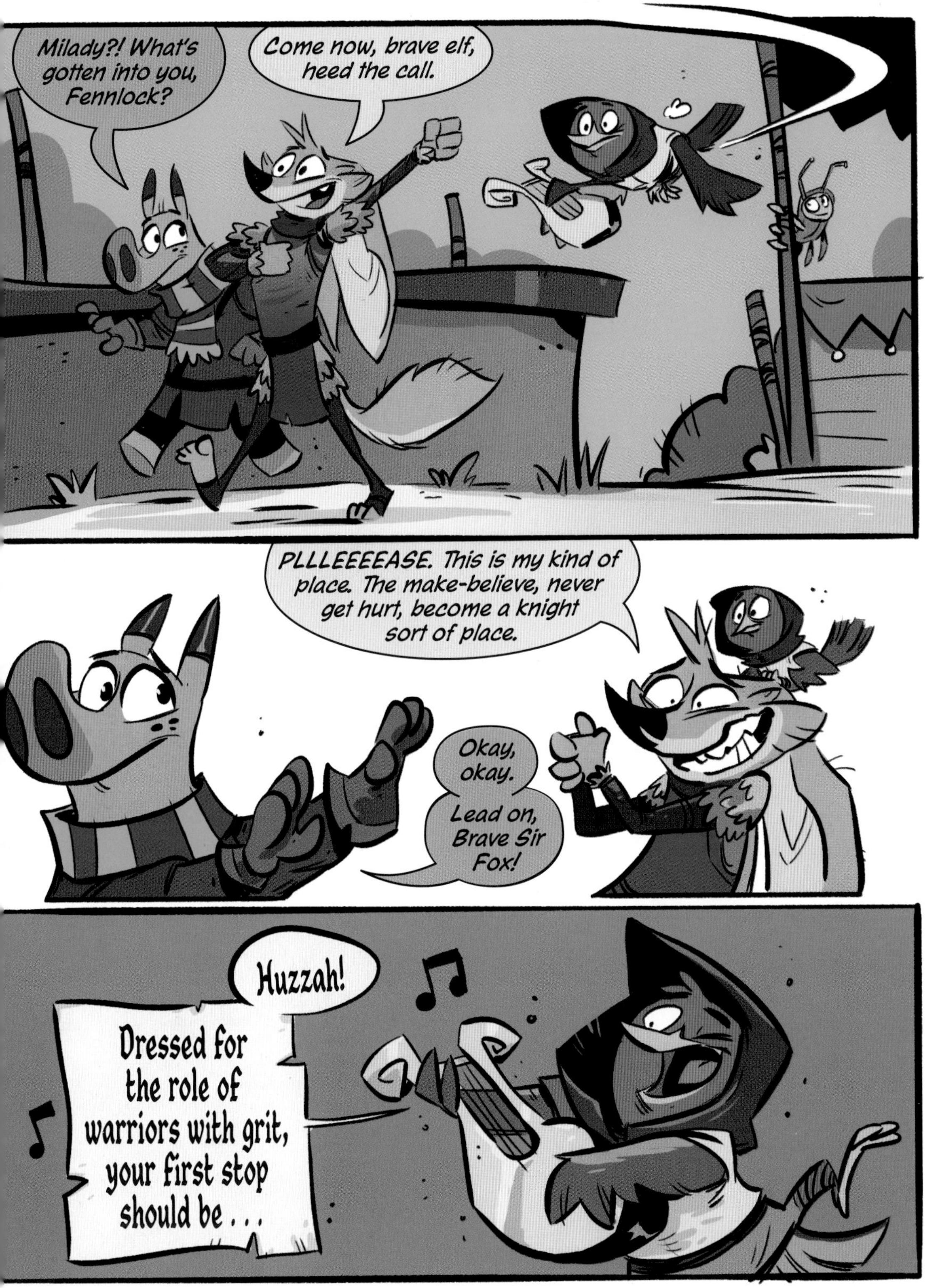
Milady?! What's gotten into you, Fennlock?
Come now, brave elf, heed the call.
PLLLEEEEASE. This is my kind of place. The make-believe, never get hurt, become a knight sort of place.
Okay, okay.
Lead on, Brave Sir Fox!
Huzzah!
Dressed for the role of warriors with grit, your first stop should be . . .

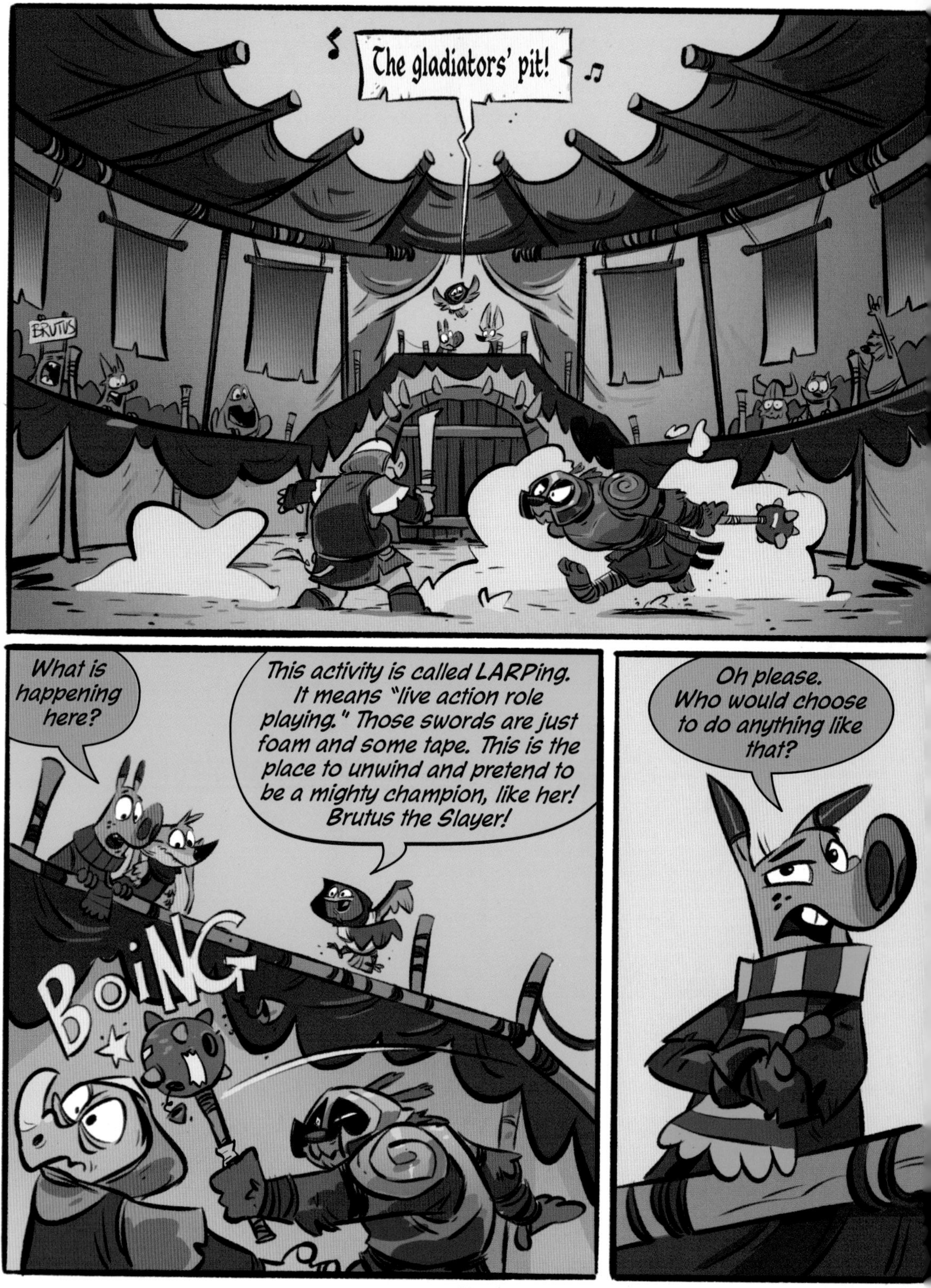
The gladiators' pit!
BRUTUS
What is happening here?
This activity is called LARPing. It means "live action role playing." Those swords are just foam and some tape. This is the place to unwind and pretend to be a mighty champion, like her! Brutus the Slayer!
BOiNG
Oh please. Who would choose to do anything like that?

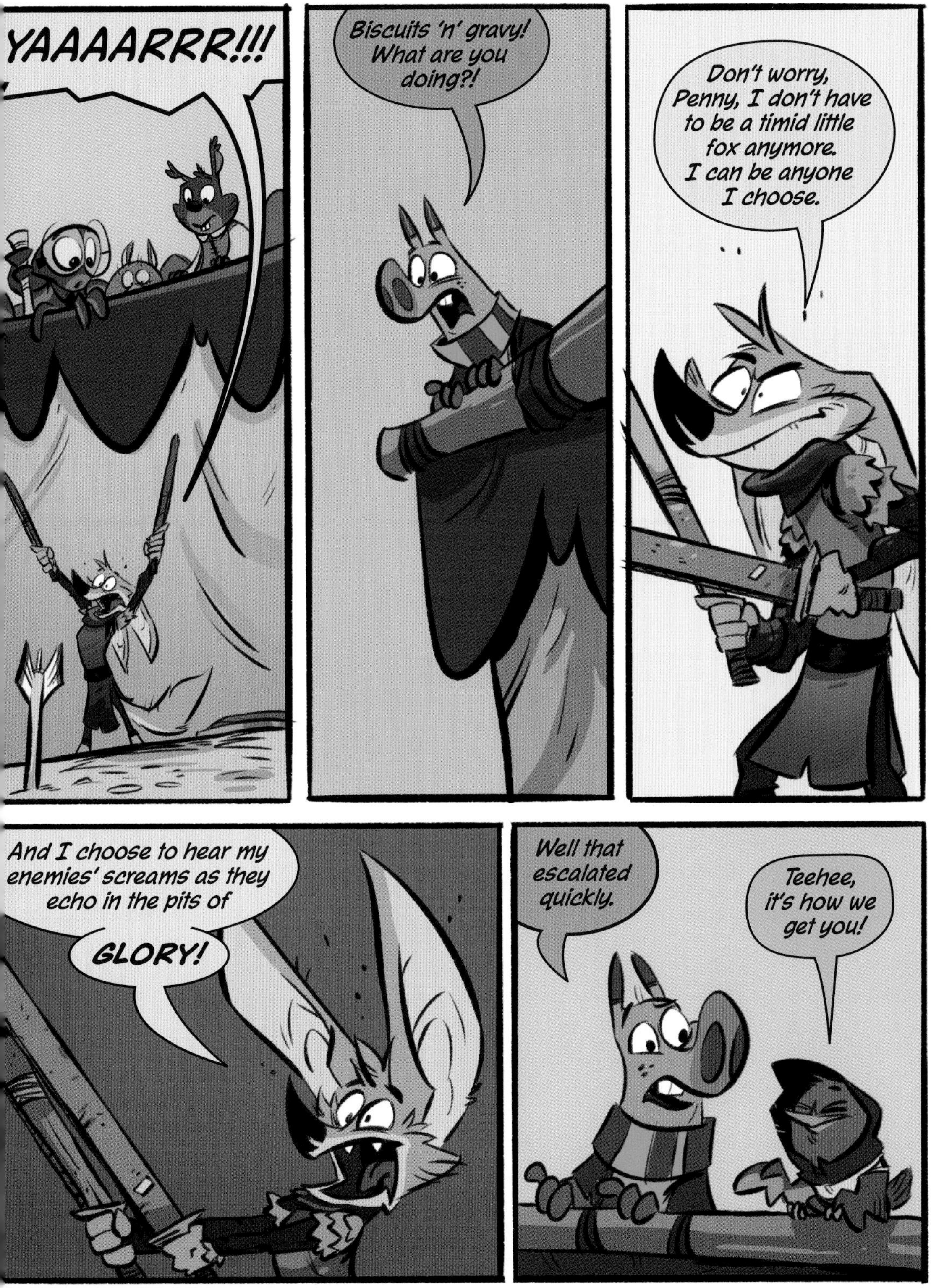
YAAAARRR!!!
Biscuits 'n' gravy! What are you doing?!
Don't worry, Penny, I don't have to be a timid little fox anymore. I can be anyone I choose.
And I choose to hear my enemies' screams as they echo in the pits of
GLORY!
Well that escalated quickly.
Teehee, it's how we get you!

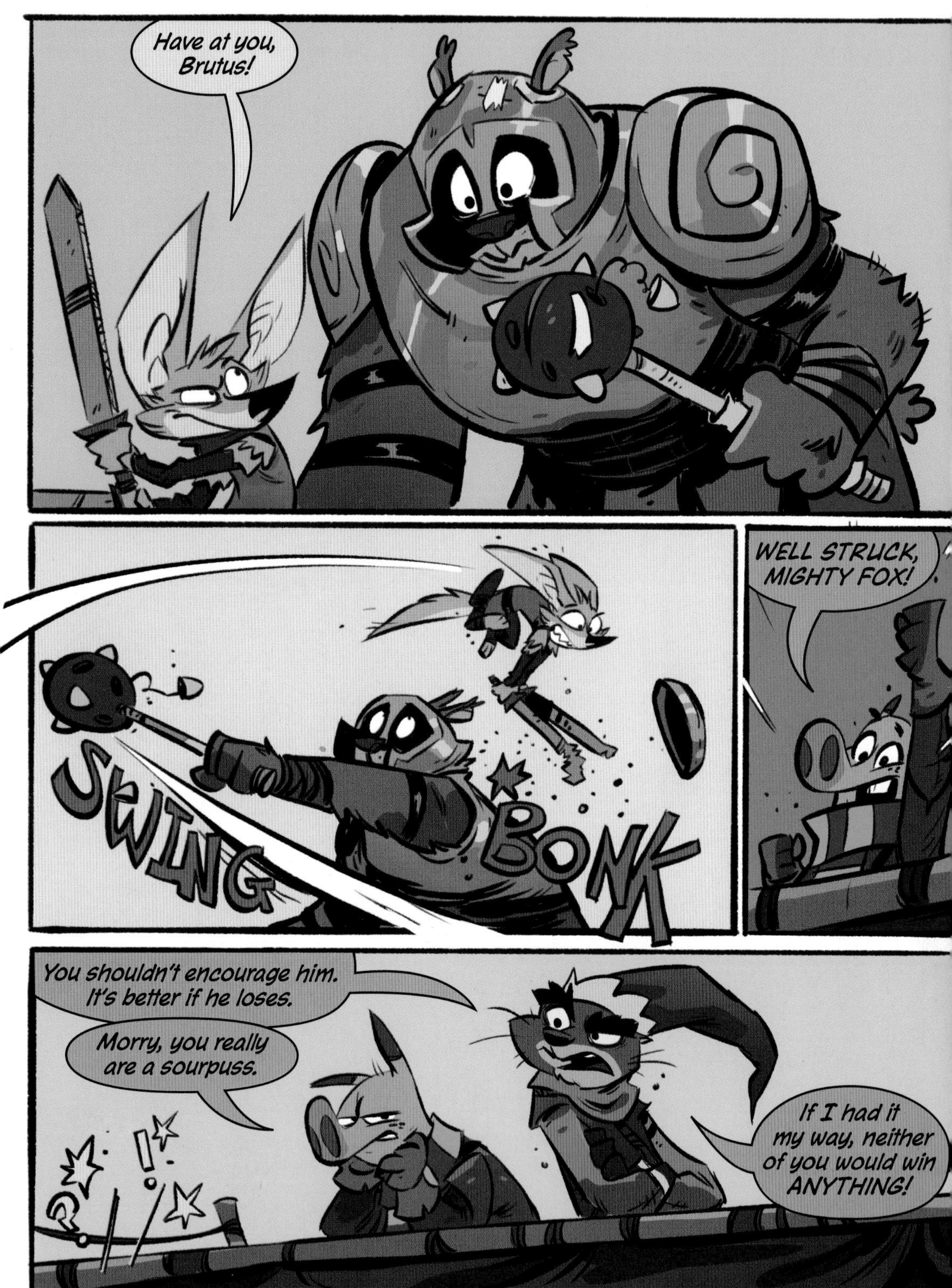

Have at you, Brutus!
SWING
BONK
WELL STRUCK, MIGHTY FOX!
You shouldn't encourage him. It's better if he loses.
Morry, you really are a sourpuss.
If I had it my way, neither of you would win ANYTHING!

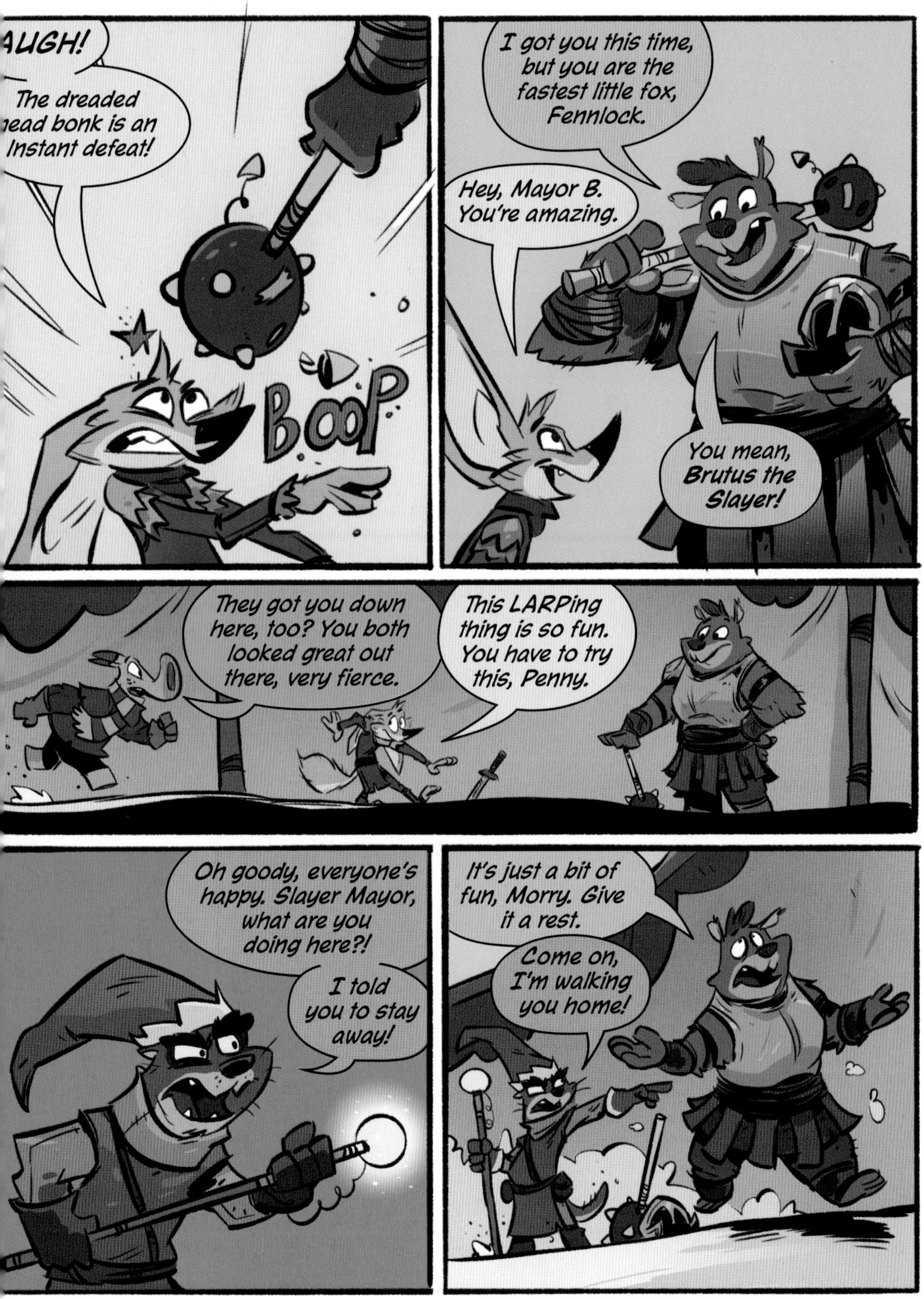
AUGH!
The dreaded head bonk is an Instant defeat!
BOOP
I got you this time, but you are the fastest little fox, Fennlock.
Hey, Mayor B. You're amazing.
You mean, Brutus the Slayer!
They got you down here, too? You both looked great out there, very fierce.
This LARPing thing is so fun. You have to try this, Penny.
Oh goody, everyone's happy. Slayer Mayor, what are you doing here?!
I told you to stay away!
It's just a bit of fun, Morry. Give it a rest.
Come on, I'm walking you home!

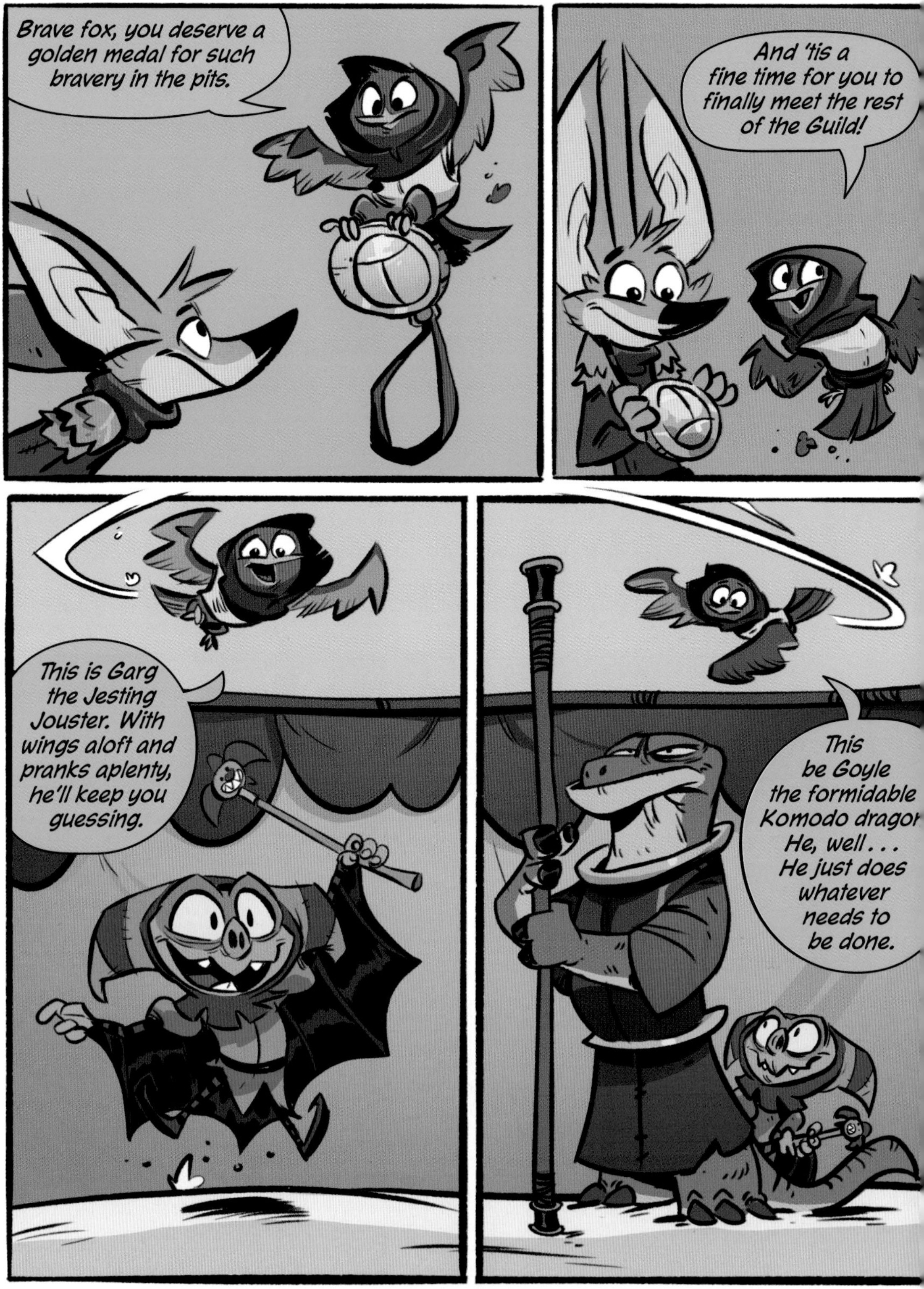
Brave fox, you deserve a golden medal for such bravery in the pits.
And 'tis a fine time for you to finally meet the rest of the Guild!
This is Garg the Jesting Jouster. With wings aloft and pranks aplenty, he'll keep you guessing.
This be Goyle the formidable Komodo dragon. He, well . . . He just does whatever needs to be done.

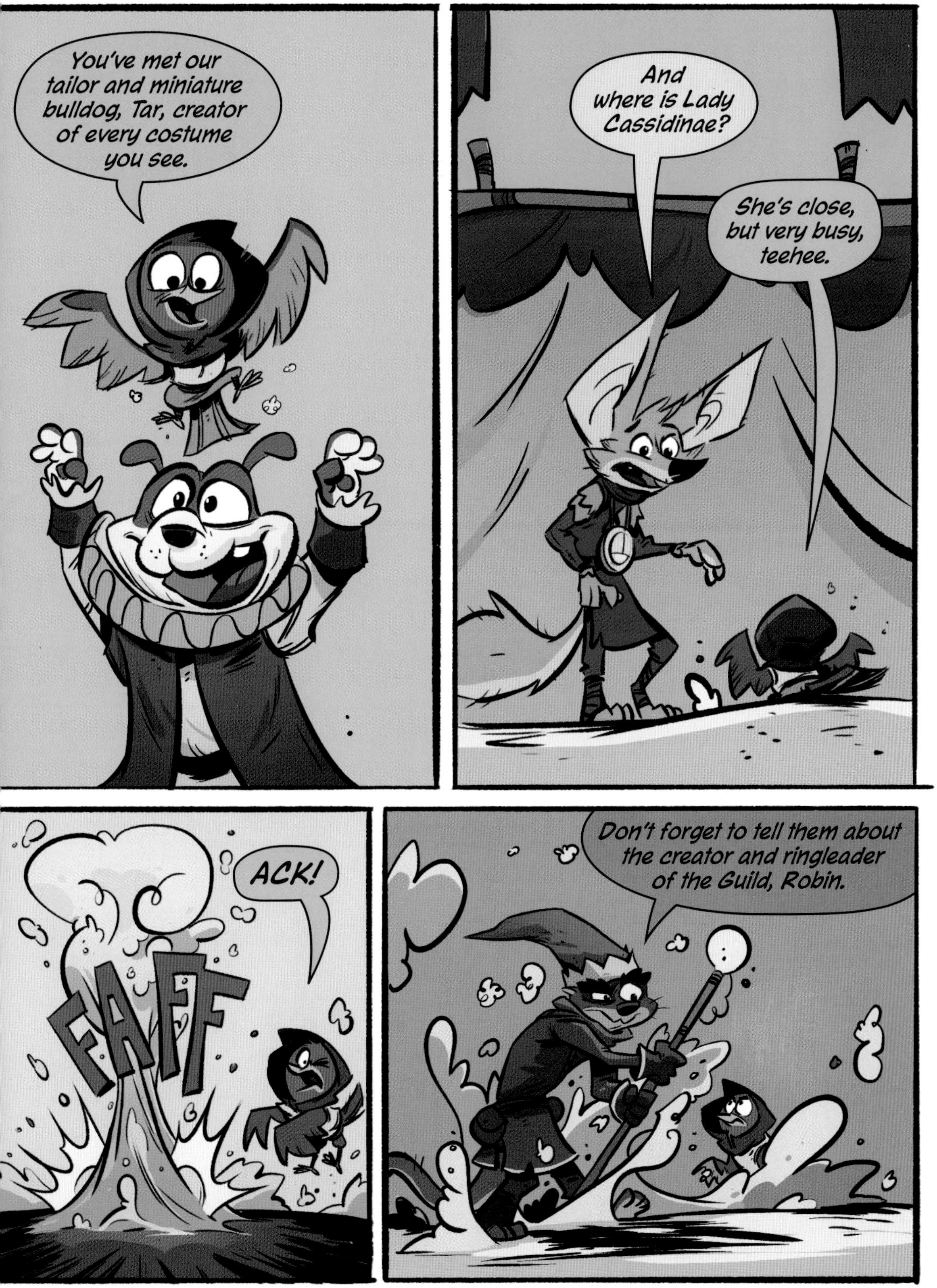
You've met our tailor and miniature bulldog, Tar, creator of every costume you see.
And where is Lady Cassidinae?
She's close, but very busy, teehee.
ACK!
FAFF
Don't forget to tell them about the creator and ringleader of the Guild, Robin.

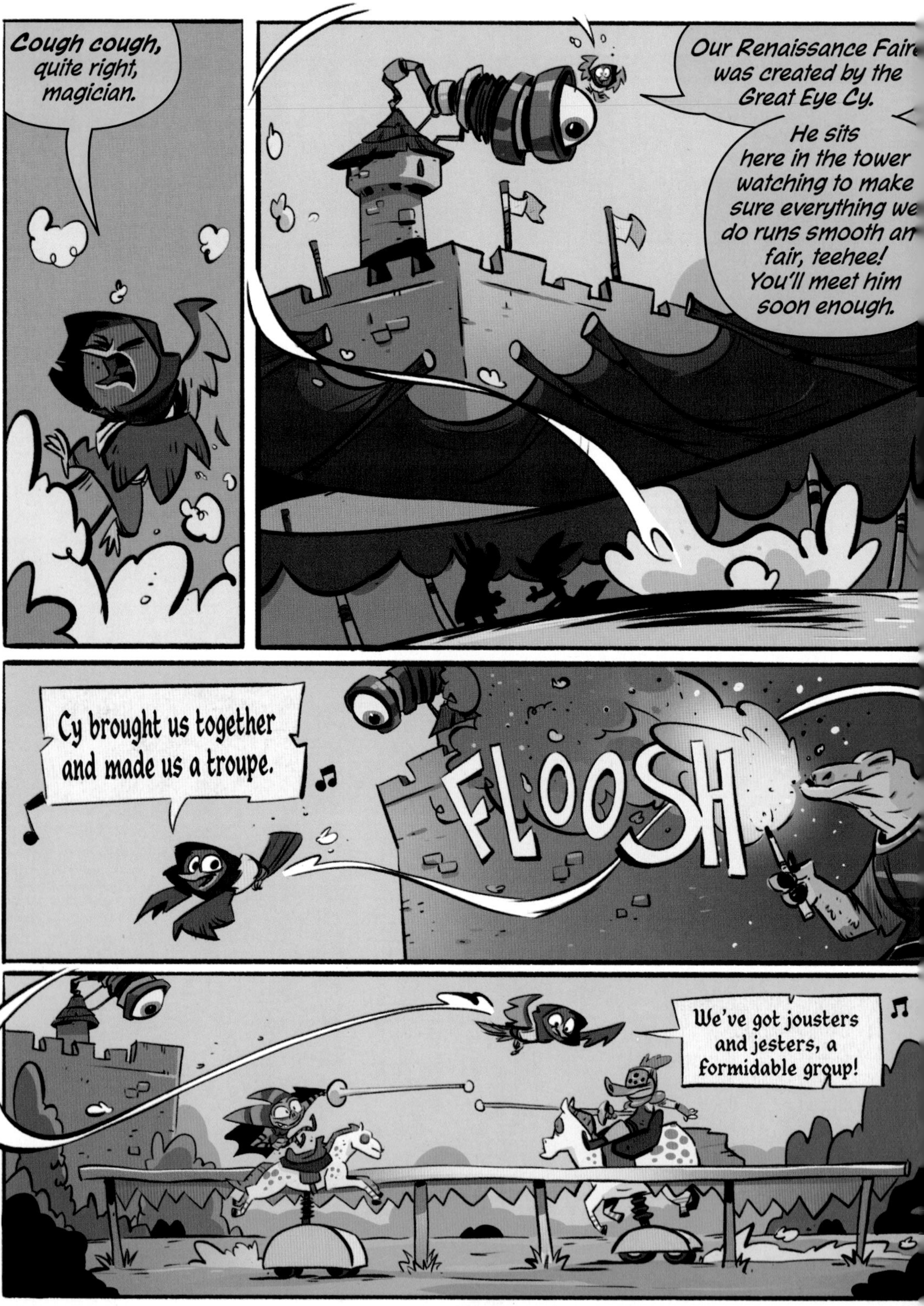
Cough cough, quite right, magician.
Our Renaissance Fair was created by the Great Eye Cy.
He sits here in the tower watching to make sure everything we do runs smooth an fair, teehee! You'll meet him soon enough.
Cy brought us together and made us a troupe.
FLOOSH
We've got jousters and jesters, a formidable group!

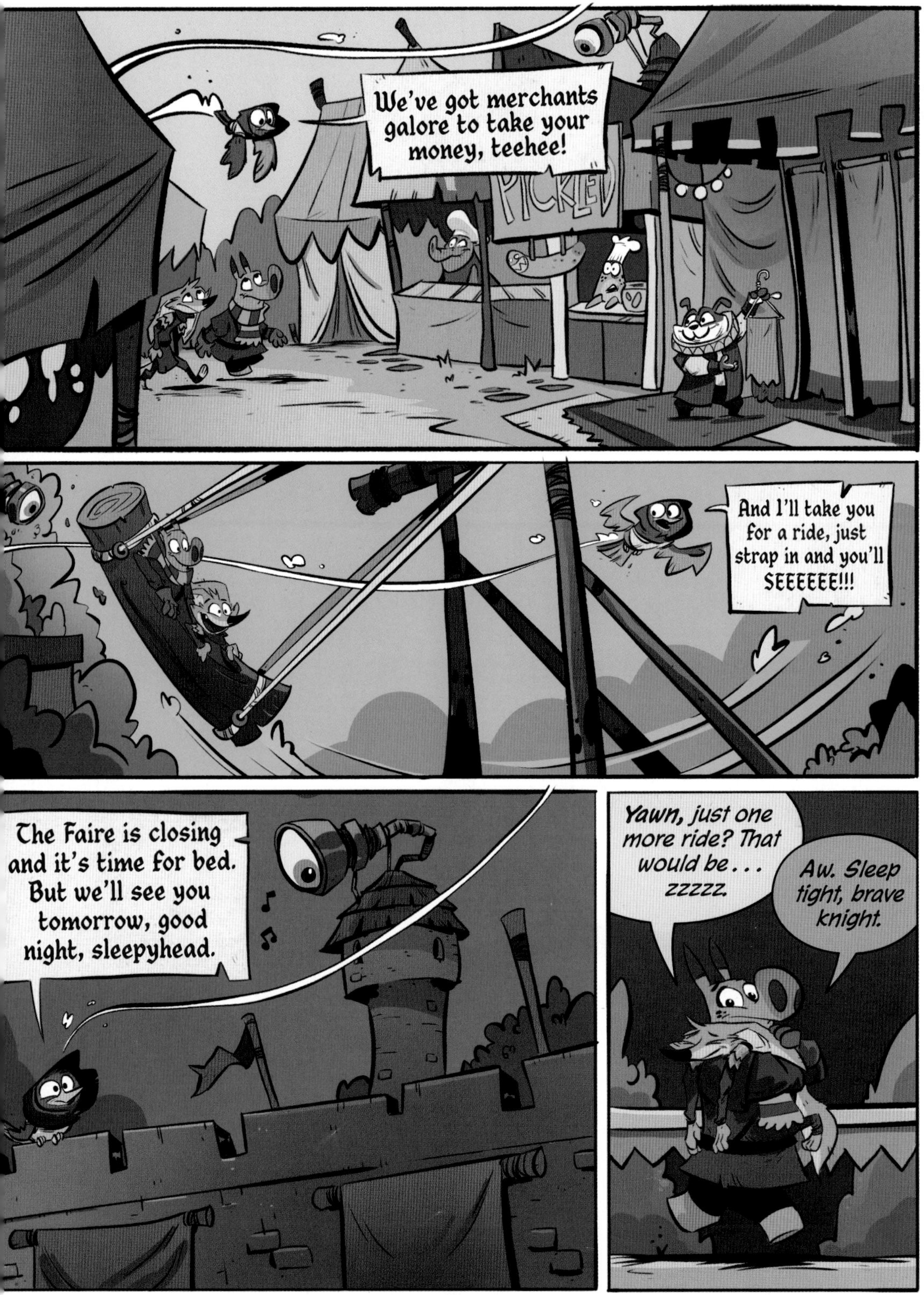
We've got merchants galore to take your money, teehee!
PICKLED
And I'll take you for a ride, just strap in and you'll SEEEEEE!!!
The Faire is closing and it's time for bed. But we'll see you tomorrow, good night, sleepyhead.
Yawn, just one more ride? That would be . . . zzzzz.
Aw. Sleep tight, brave knight.

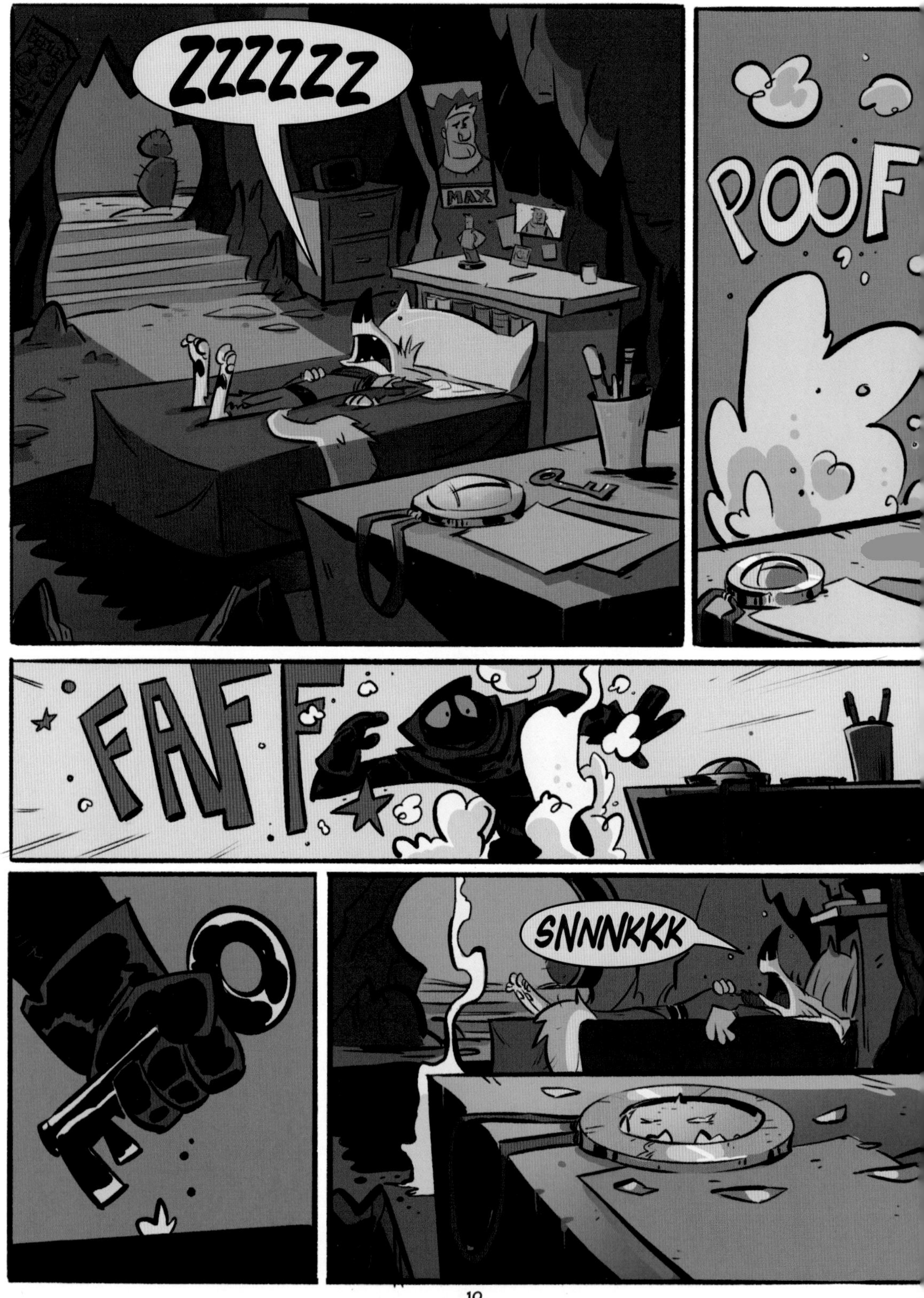
ZZZZZZ
MAX
POOF
FAFF
SNNNKKK

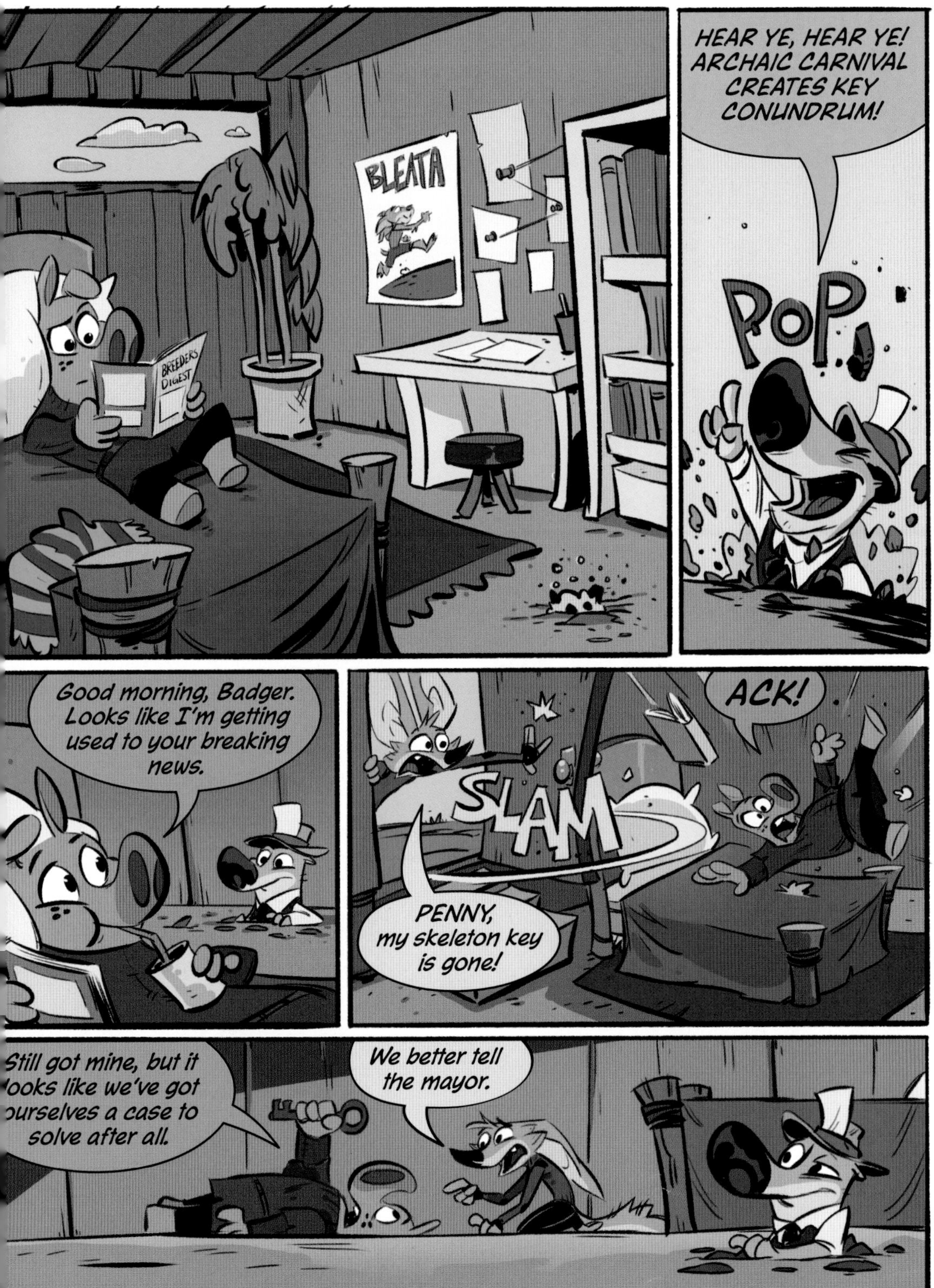
BLEATA
BREEDERS DIGEST
HEAR YE, HEAR YE! ARCHAIC CARNIVAL CREATES KEY CONUNDRUM!
POP
Good morning, Badger. Looks like I'm getting used to your breaking news.
ACK!
SLAM
PENNY, my skeleton key is gone!
Still got mine, but it looks like we've got ourselves a case to solve after all.
We better tell the mayor.

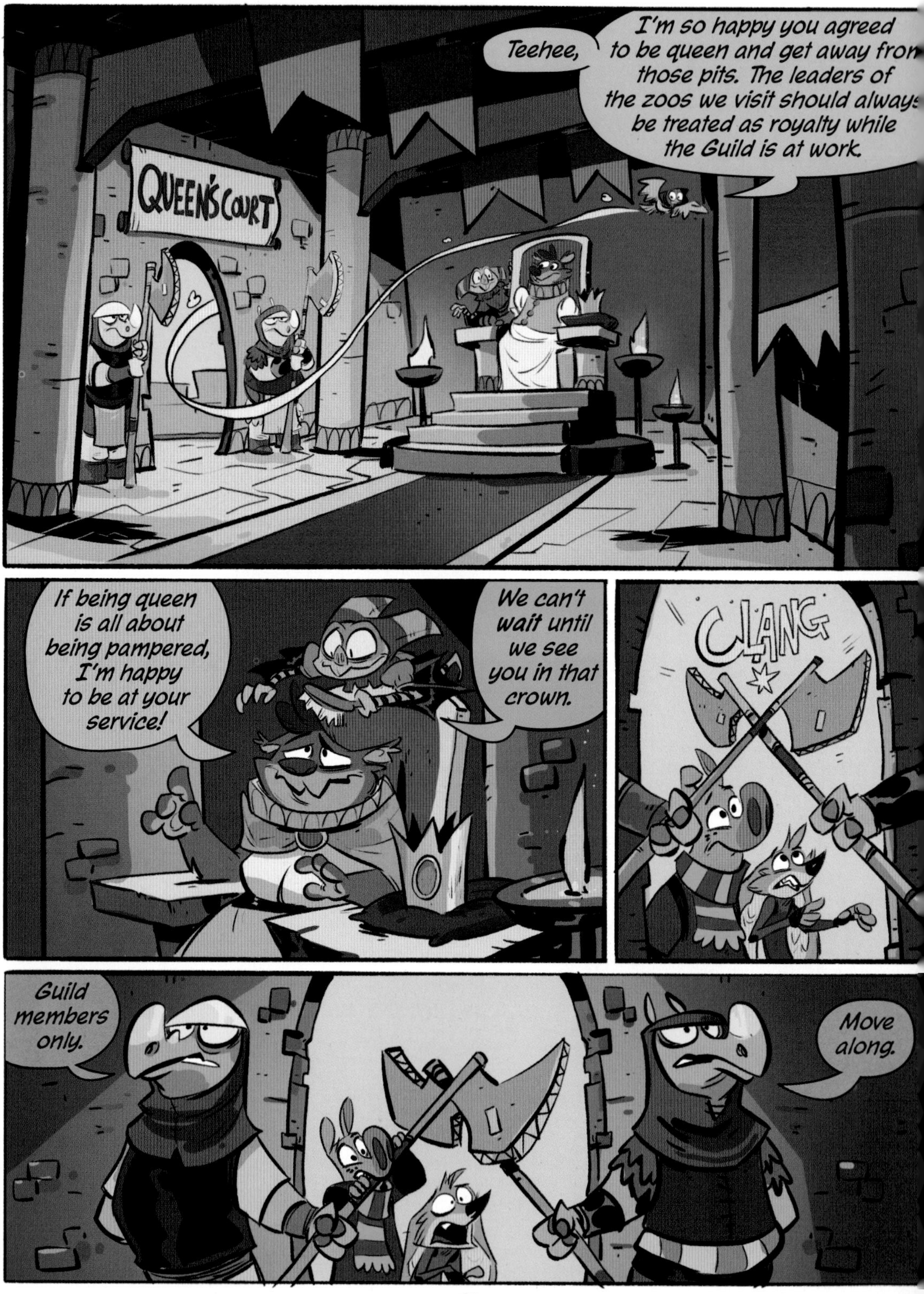
QUEEN'S COURT
Teehee,
I'm so happy you agreed to be queen and get away from those pits. The leaders of the zoos we visit should always be treated as royalty while the Guild is at work.
If being queen is all about being pampered, I'm happy to be at your service!
We can't wait until we see you in that crown.
CLANG
Guild members only.
Move along.

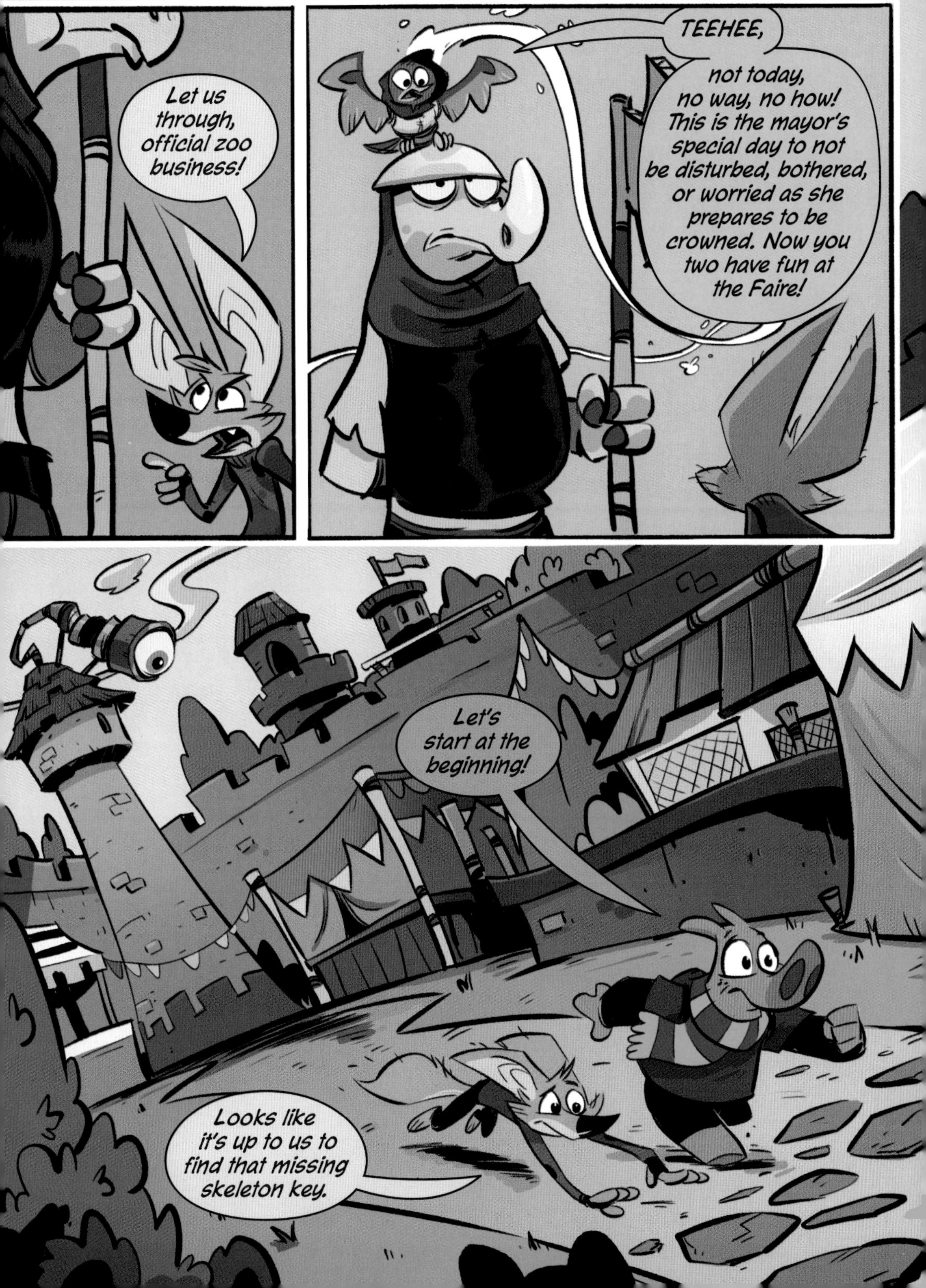
Let us through, official zoo business!
TEEHEE,
not today, no way, no how! This is the mayor's special day to not be disturbed, bothered, or worried as she prepares to be crowned. Now you two have fun at the Faire!
Let's start at the beginning!
Looks like it's up to us to find that missing skeleton key.

Hmmm, so this thief broke your medal, too. Seems rather rude.

And they left no prints, like they just magically poofed in and out of the place.

With that key, they can get into anything in Wild Zoo Yonder!

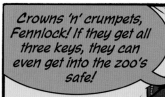

Crowns 'n' crumpets, Fennlock! If they get all three keys, they can even get into the zoo's safe!

GASP, that's where Mayor Big Bear keeps our most valuable possessions, even the deed to the zoo. We CAN'T lose our other key now!

Easier said than done.

What the?

Who the?!

22

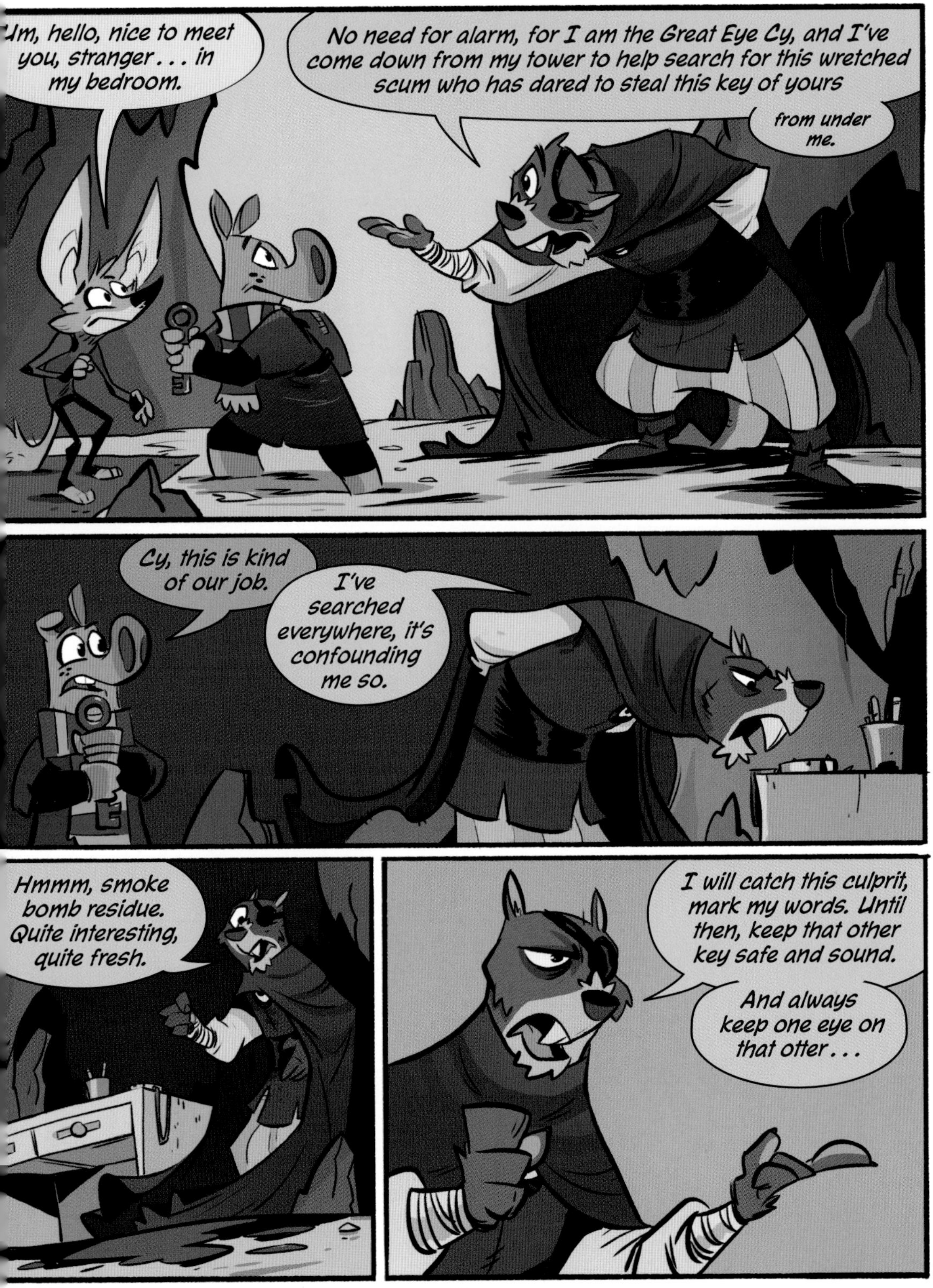
Um, hello, nice to meet you, stranger . . . in my bedroom.
No need for alarm, for I am the Great Eye Cy, and I've come down from my tower to help search for this wretched scum who has dared to steal this key of yours
from under me.
Cy, this is kind of our job.
I've searched everywhere, it's confounding me so.
Hmmm, smoke bomb residue. Quite interesting, quite fresh.
I will catch this culprit, mark my words. Until then, keep that other key safe and sound.
And always keep one eye on that otter . . .

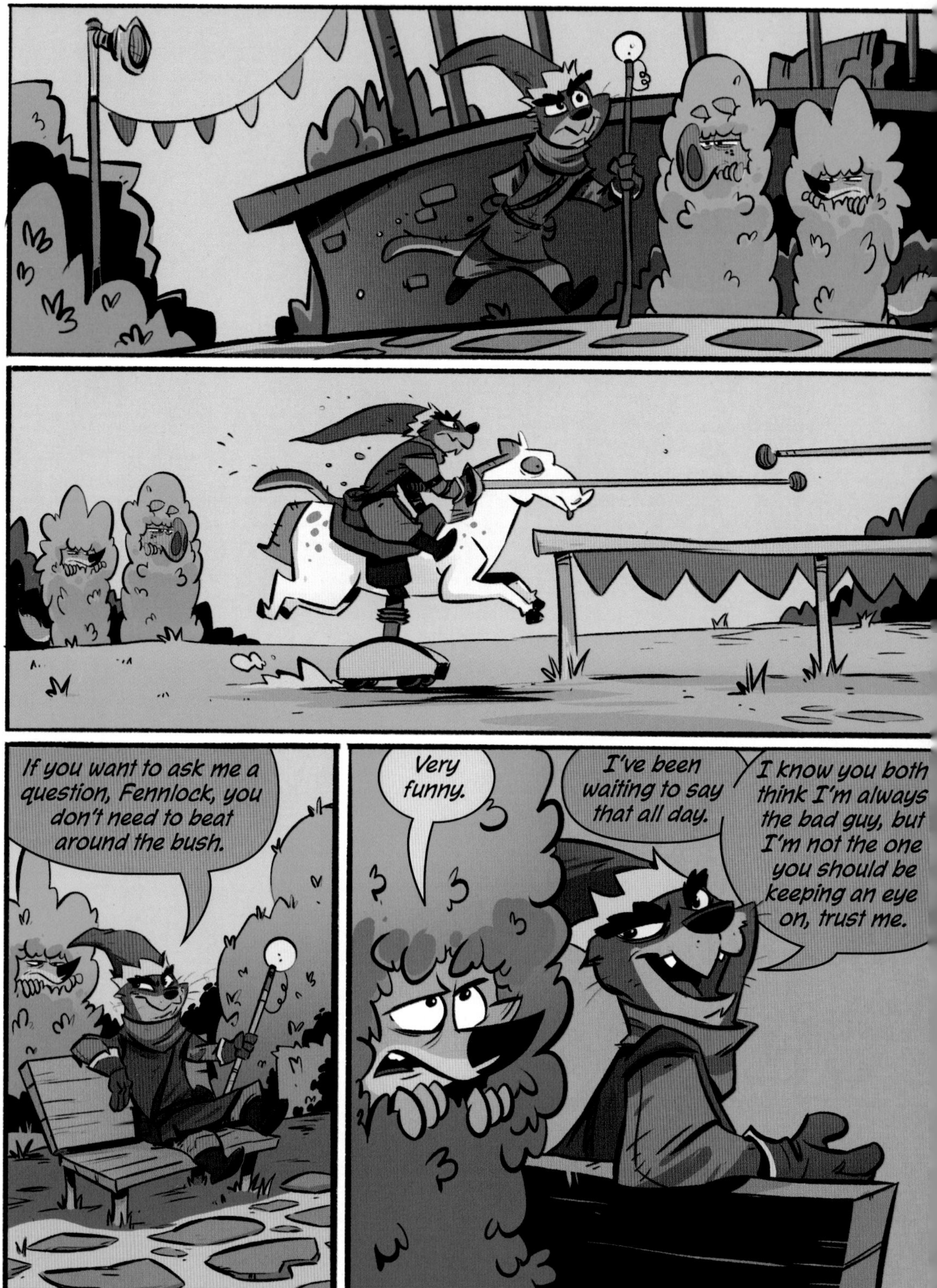
If you want to ask me a question, Fennlock, you don't need to beat around the bush.
Very funny.
I've been waiting to say that all day.
I know you both think I'm always the bad guy, but I'm not the one you should be keeping an eye on, trust me.

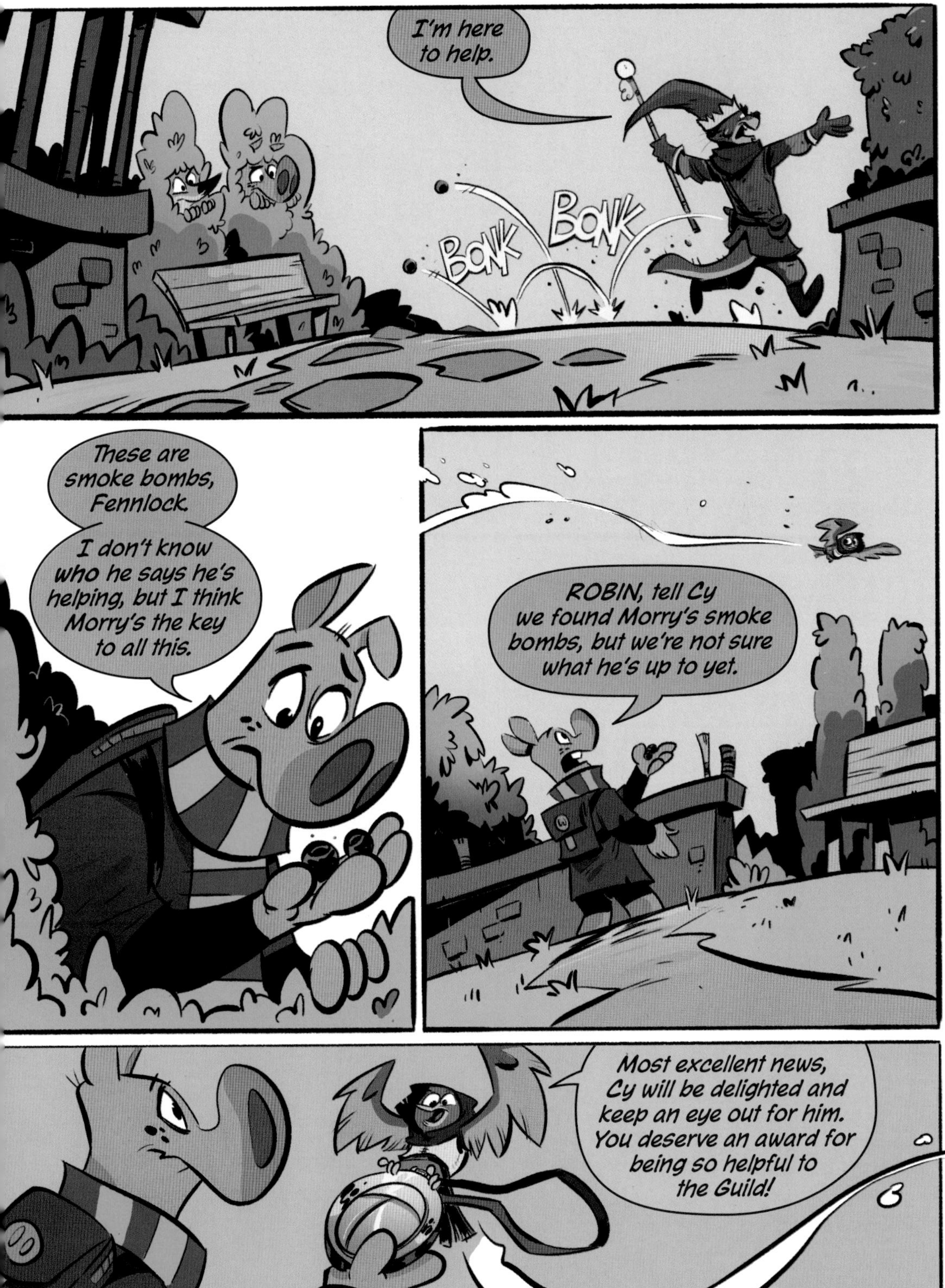
I'm here to help.
BONK
BONK
These are smoke bombs, Fennlock.
I don't know who he says he's helping, but I think Morry's the key to all this.
ROBIN, tell Cy we found Morry's smoke bombs, but we're not sure what he's up to yet.
Most excellent news, Cy will be delighted and keep an eye out for him. You deserve an award for being so helpful to the Guild!

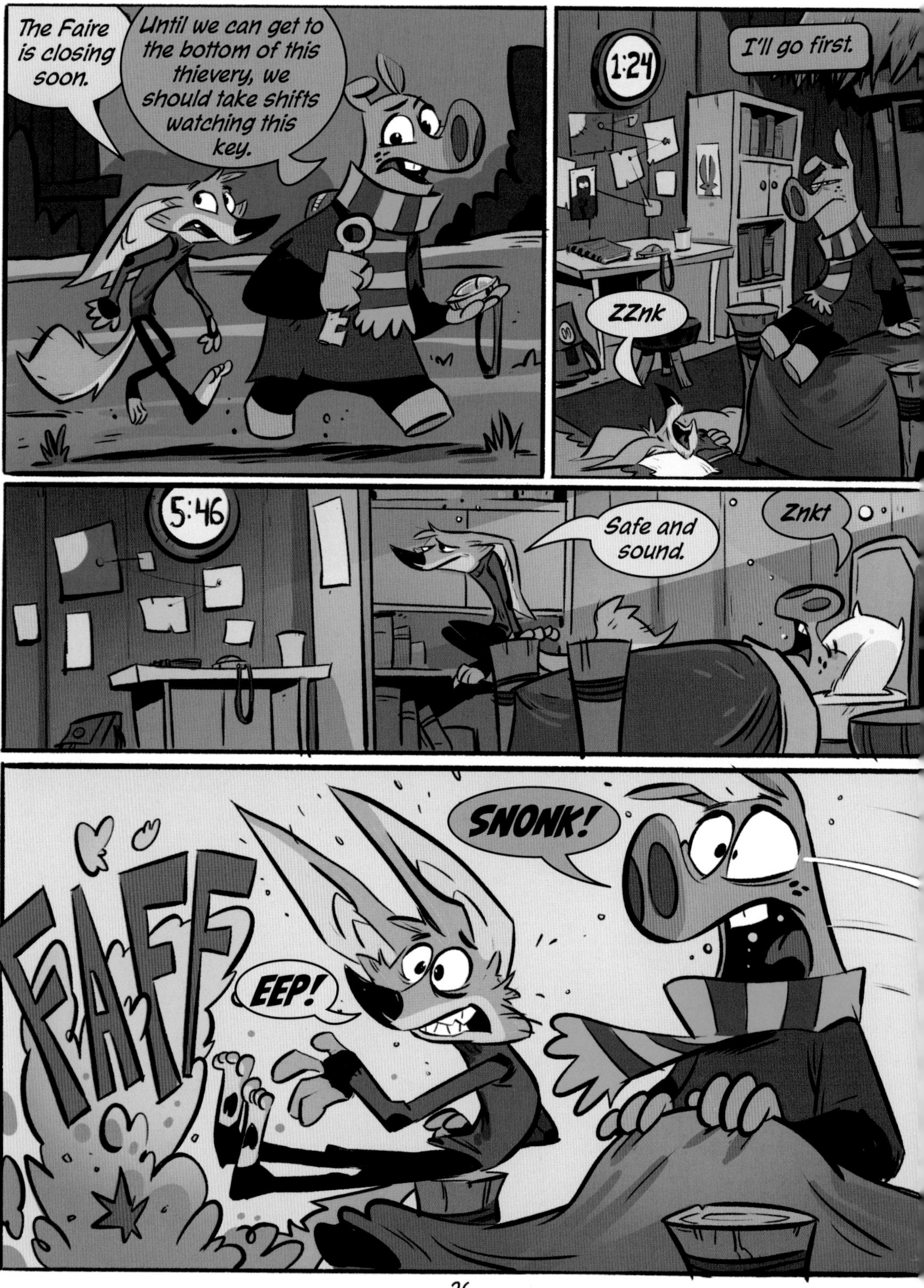
The Faire is closing soon.
Until we can get to the bottom of this thievery, we should take shifts watching this key.
1:24
I'll go first.
ZZnk
5:46
Safe and sound.
Znkt
SNONK!
FAFF
EEP!

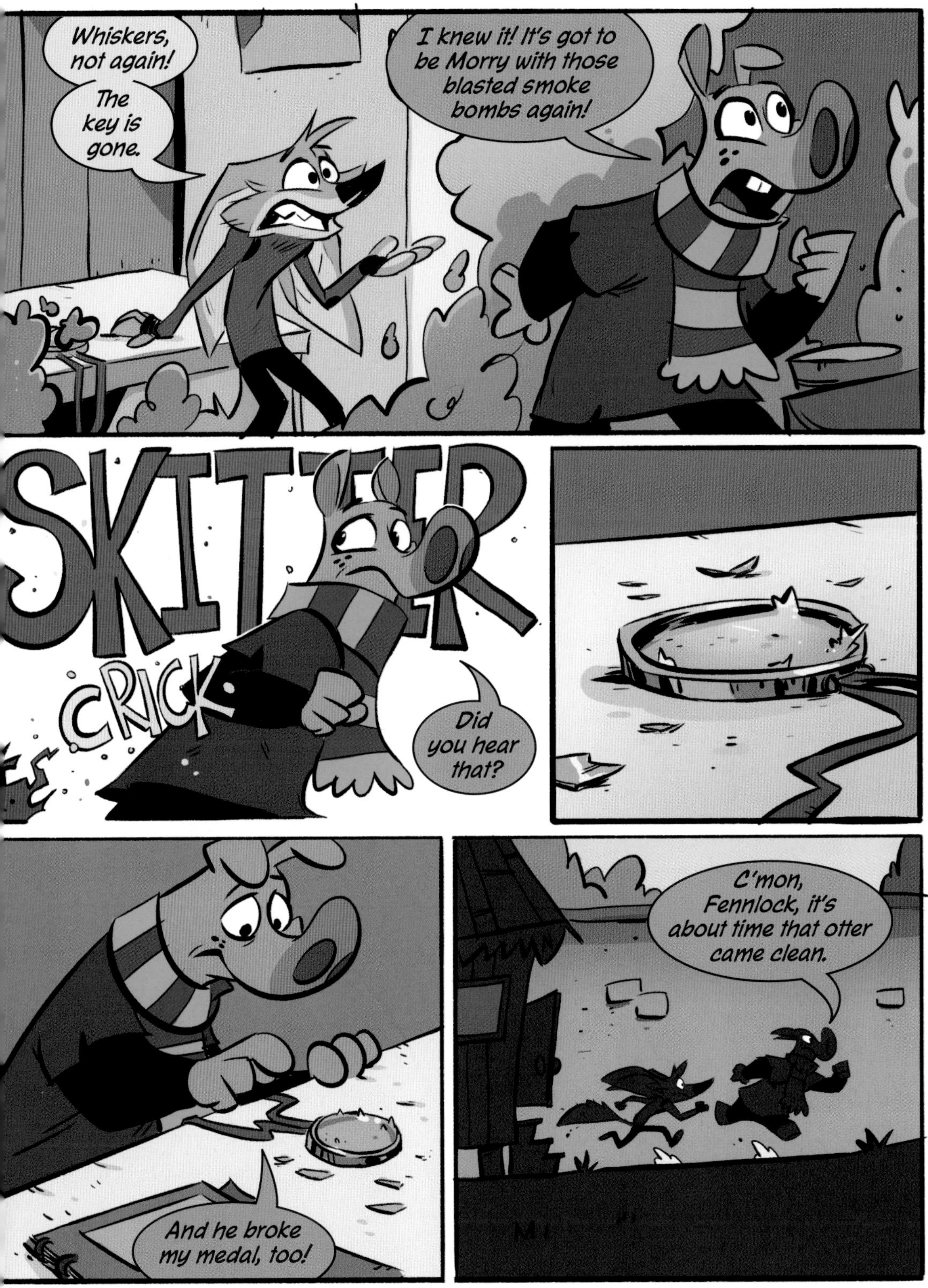
Whiskers, not again!
The key is gone.
I knew it! It's got to be Morry with those blasted smoke bombs again!
SKITTER
CRICK
Did you hear that?
And he broke my medal, too!
C'mon, Fennlock, it's about time that otter came clean.

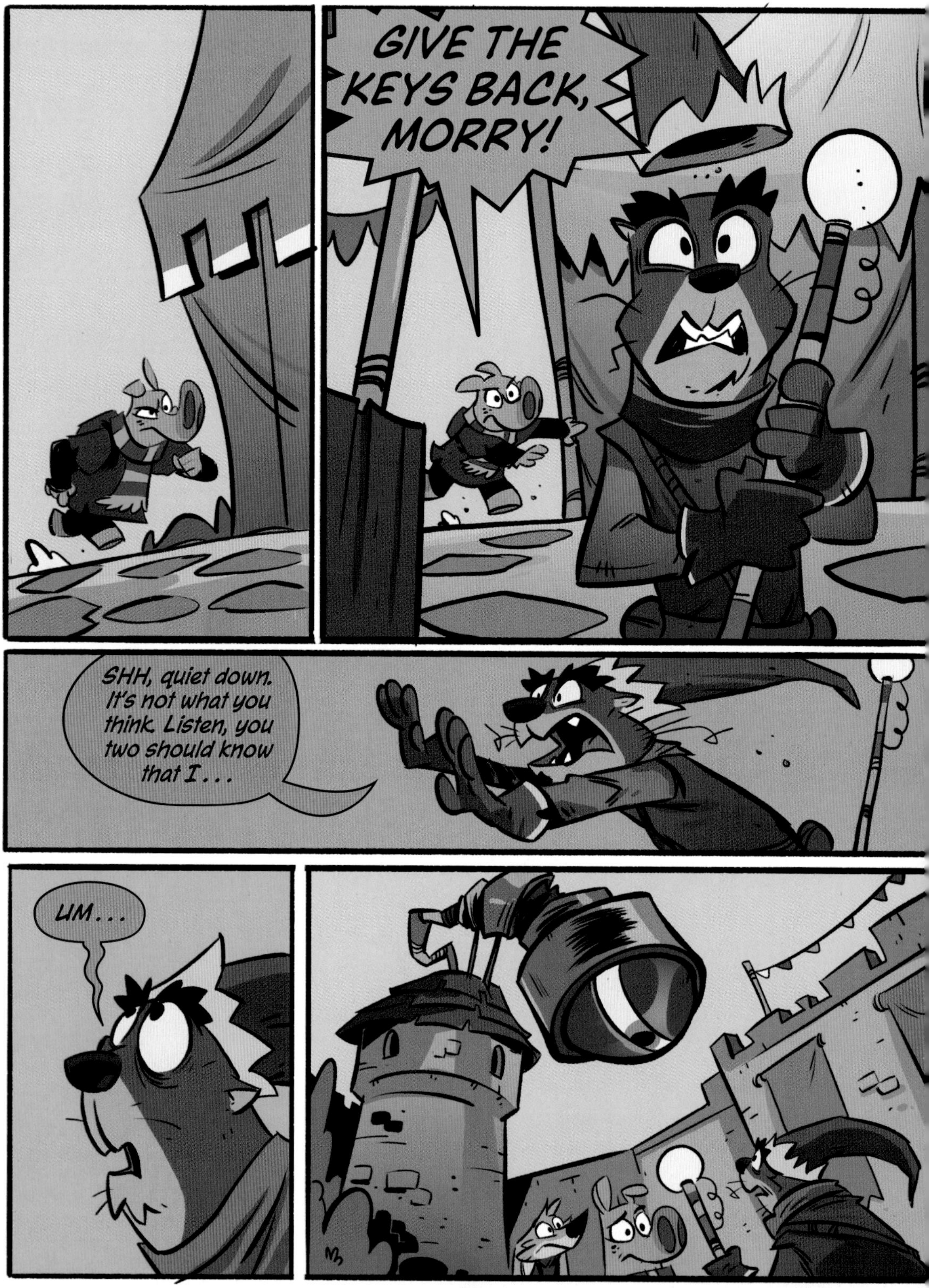
GIVE THE KEYS BACK, MORRY!
SHH, quiet down. It's not what you think. Listen, you two should know that I . . .
UM . . .

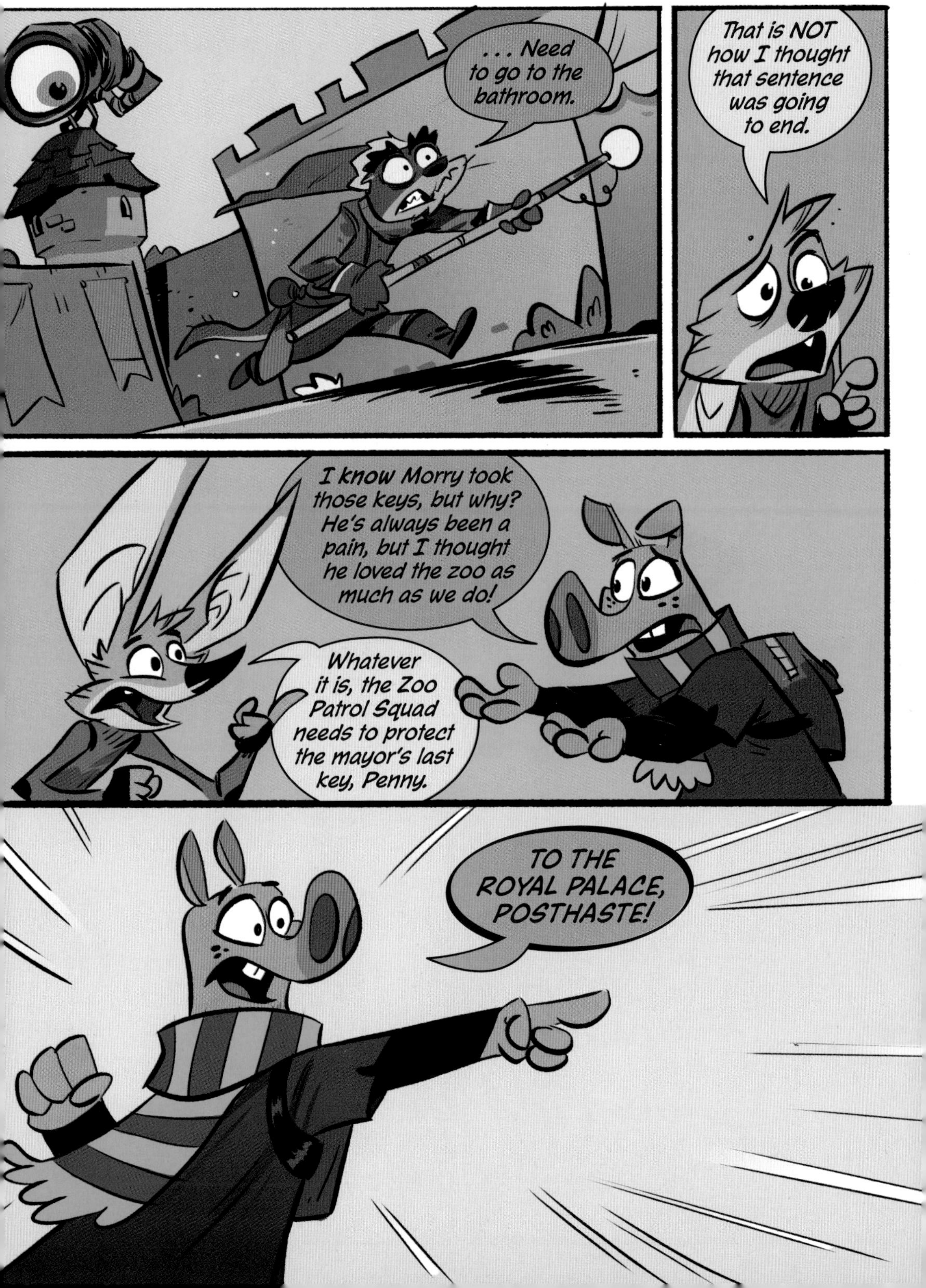
. . . Need to go to the bathroom.
That is NOT how I thought that sentence was going to end.
I know Morry took those keys, but why? He's always been a pain, but I thought he loved the zoo as much as we do!
Whatever it is, the Zoo Patrol Squad needs to protect the mayor's last key, Penny.
TO THE ROYAL PALACE, POSTHASTE!

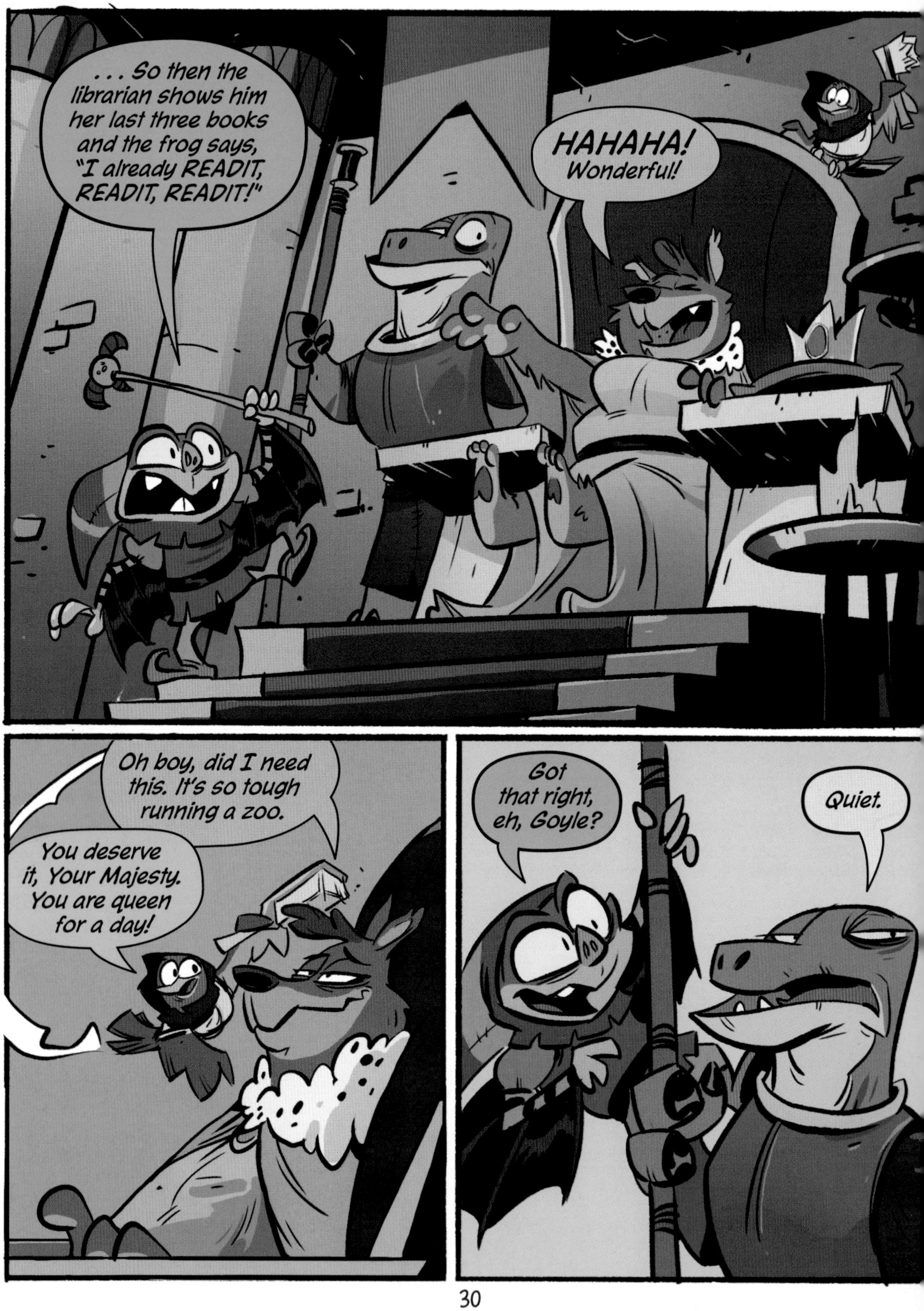
. . . So then the librarian shows him her last three books and the frog says, "I already READIT, READIT, READIT!"
HAHAHA! Wonderful!
Oh boy, did I need this. It's so tough running a zoo.
You deserve it, Your Majesty. You are queen for a day!
Got that right, eh, Goyle?
Quiet.

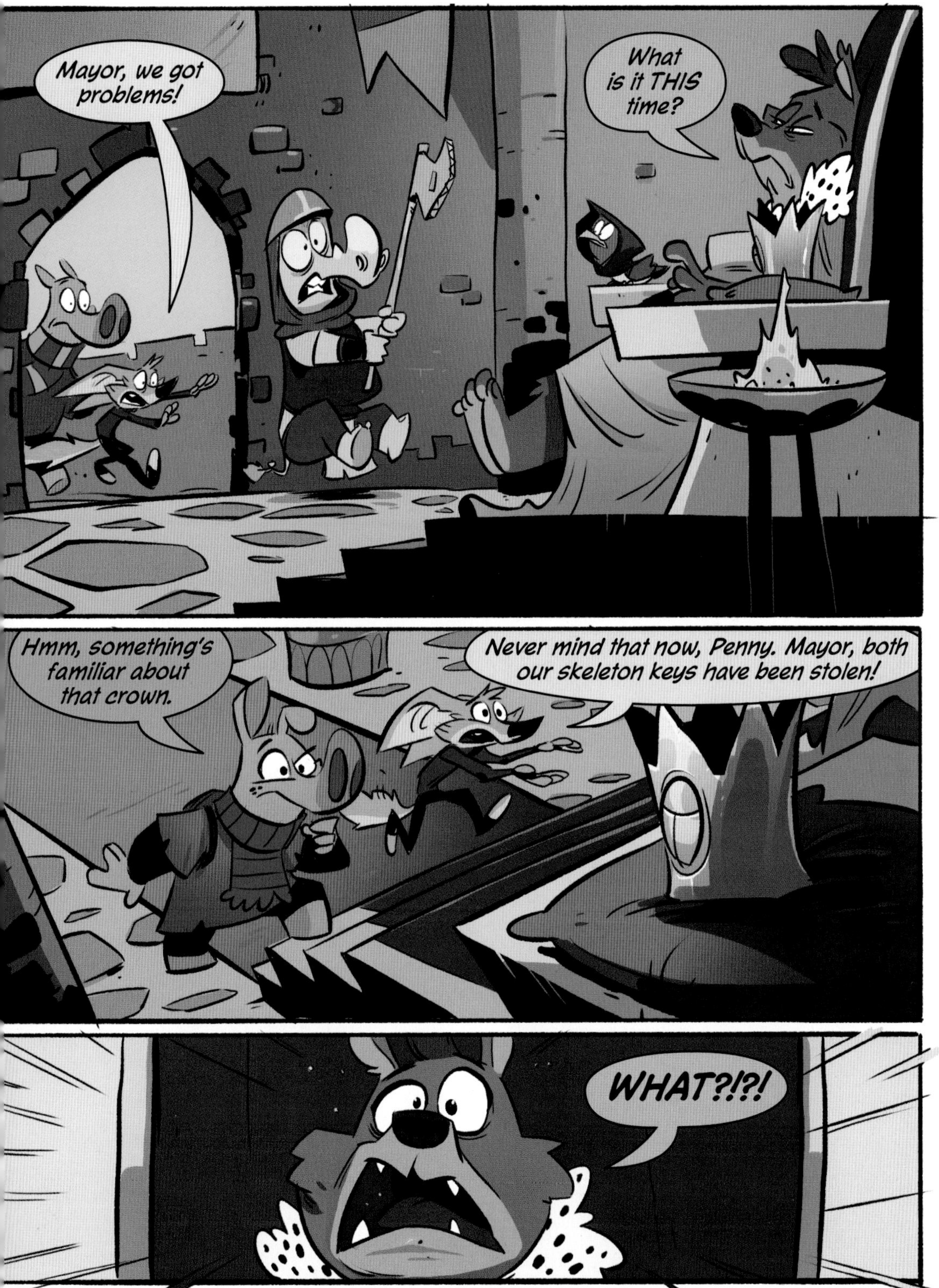
Mayor, we got problems!
What is it THIS time?
Hmm, something's familiar about that crown.
Never mind that now, Penny. Mayor, both our skeleton keys have been stolen!
WHAT?!?!

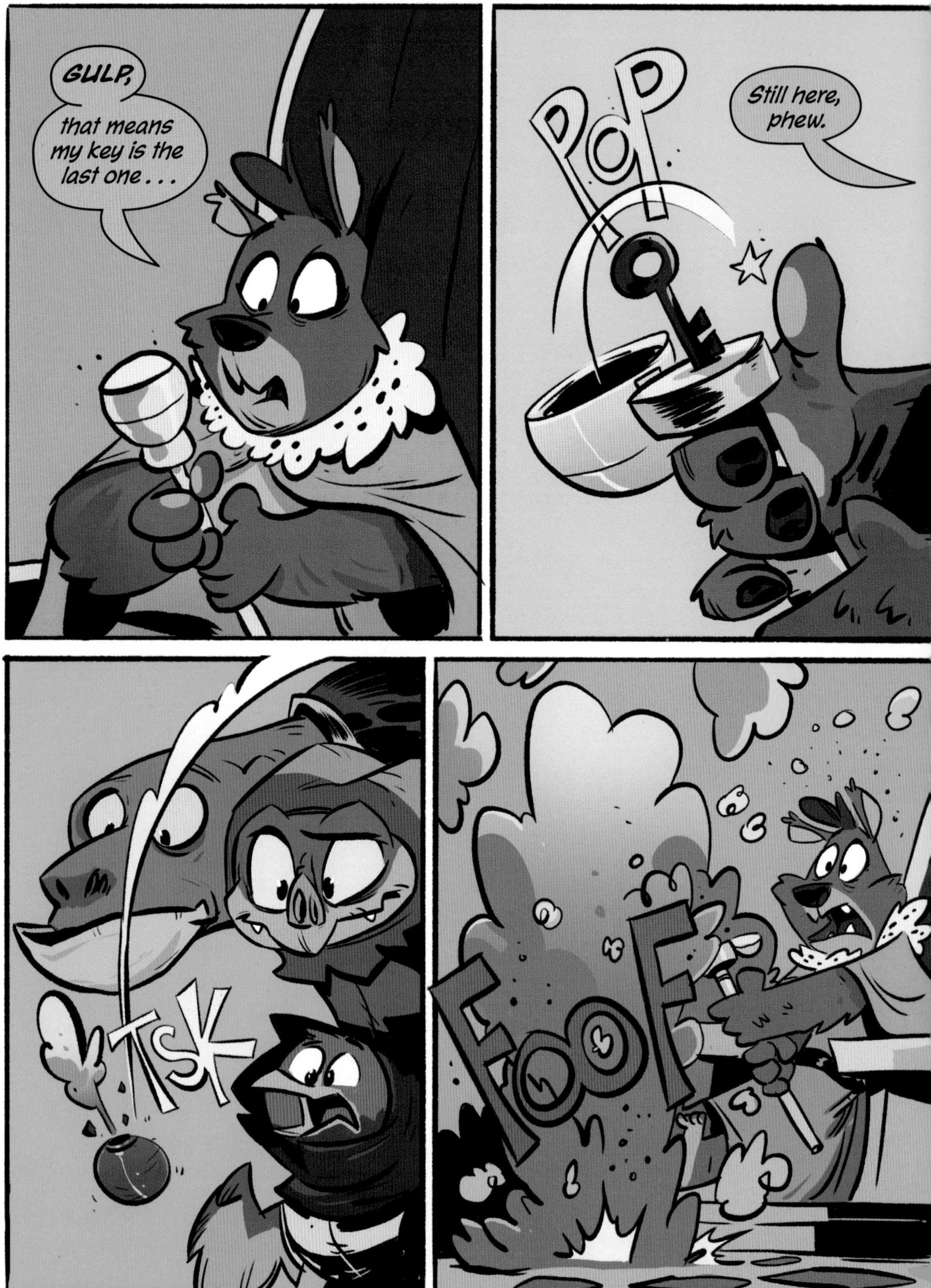
GULP,
that means my key is the last one . . .
POP
Still here, phew.
TSK
FOOF

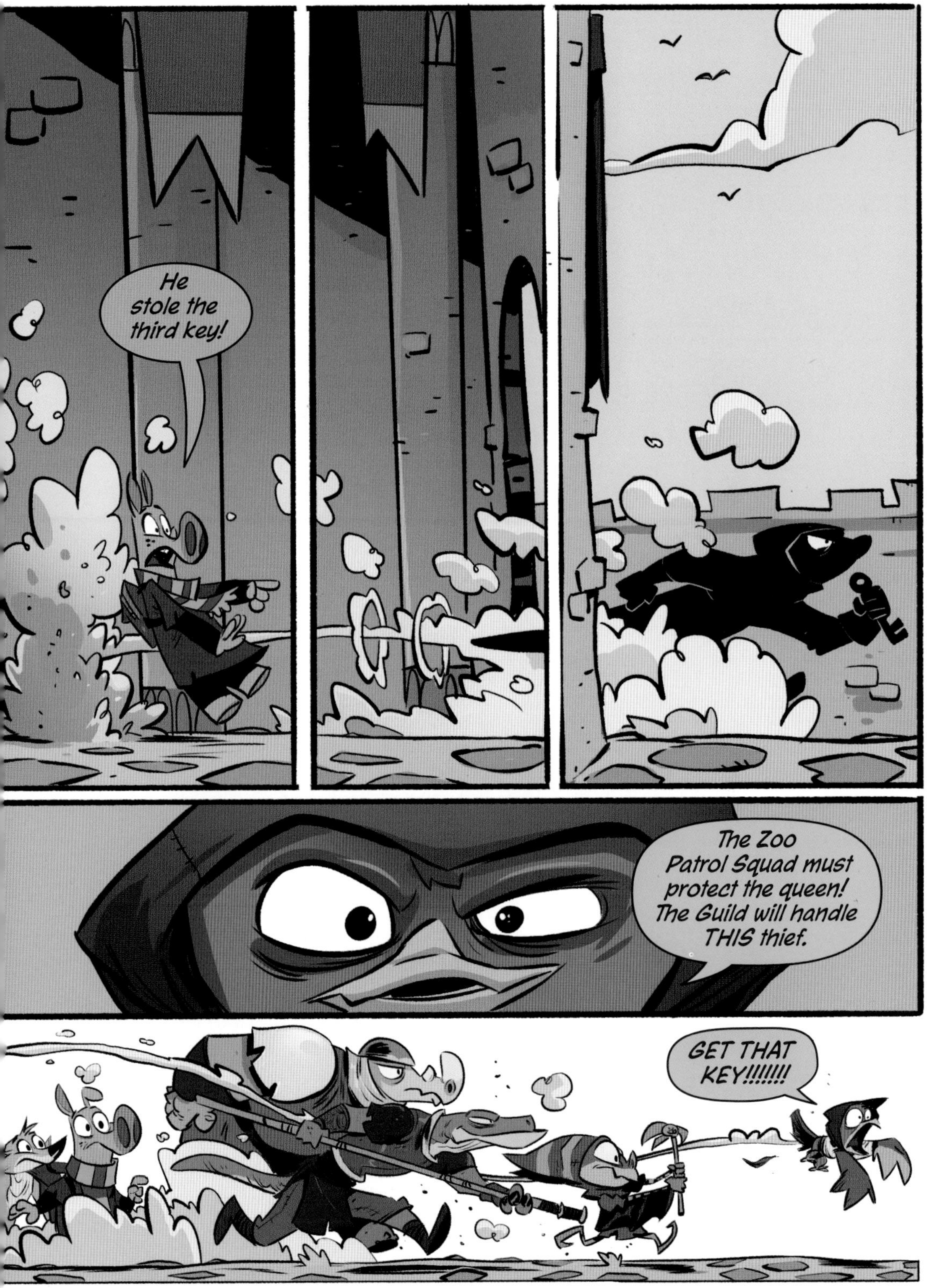
He stole the third key!
The Zoo Patrol Squad must protect the queen! The Guild will handle THIS thief.
GET THAT KEY!!!!!!!

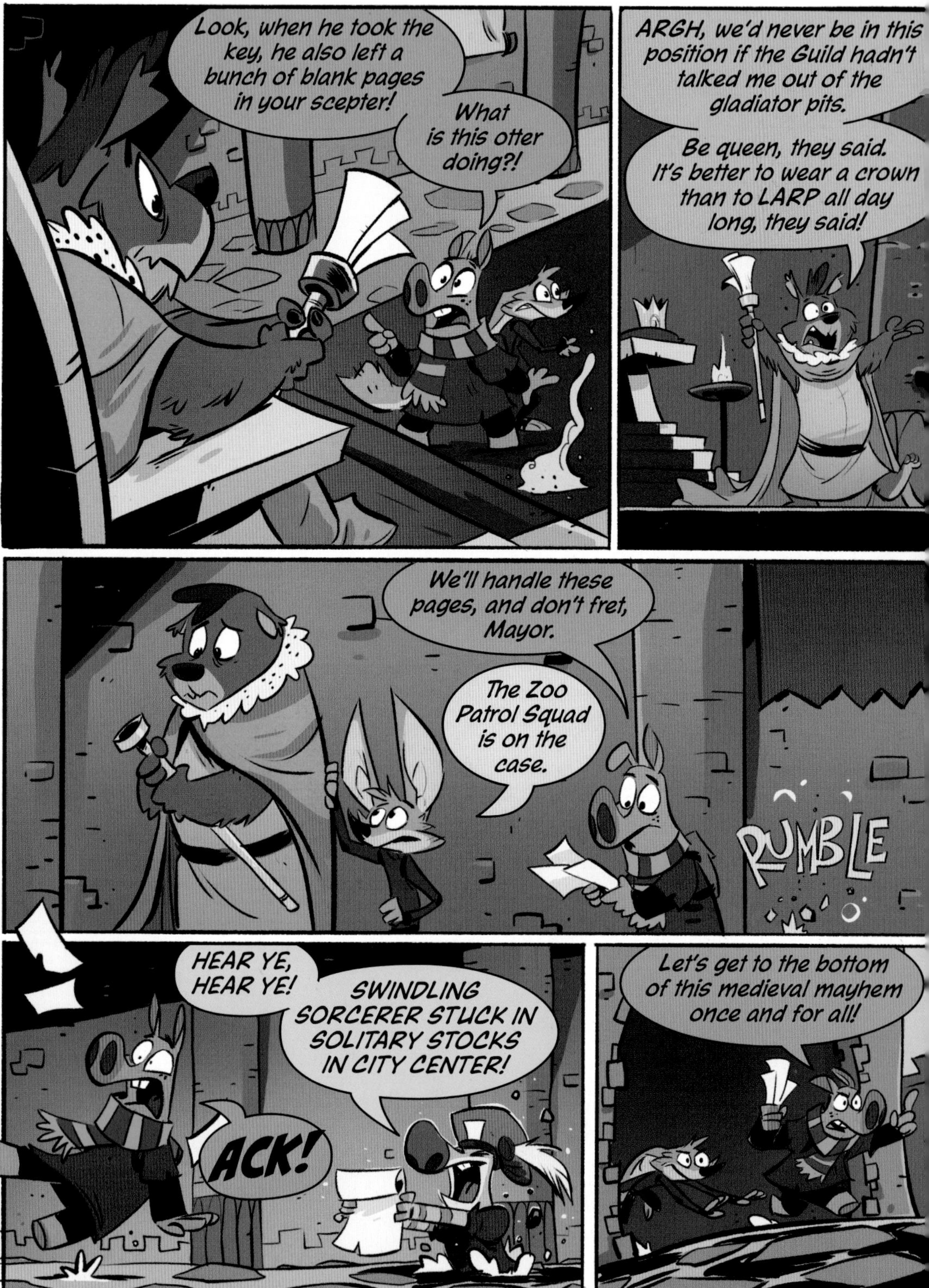
Look, when he took the key, he also left a bunch of blank pages in your scepter!
What is this otter doing?!
ARGH, we'd never be in this position if the Guild hadn't talked me out of the gladiator pits.
Be queen, they said. It's better to wear a crown than to LARP all day long, they said!
We'll handle these pages, and don't fret, Mayor.
The Zoo Patrol Squad is on the case.
RUMBLE
HEAR YE, HEAR YE!
SWINDLING SORCERER STUCK IN SOLITARY STOCKS IN CITY CENTER!
ACK!
Let's get to the bottom of this medieval mayhem once and for all!

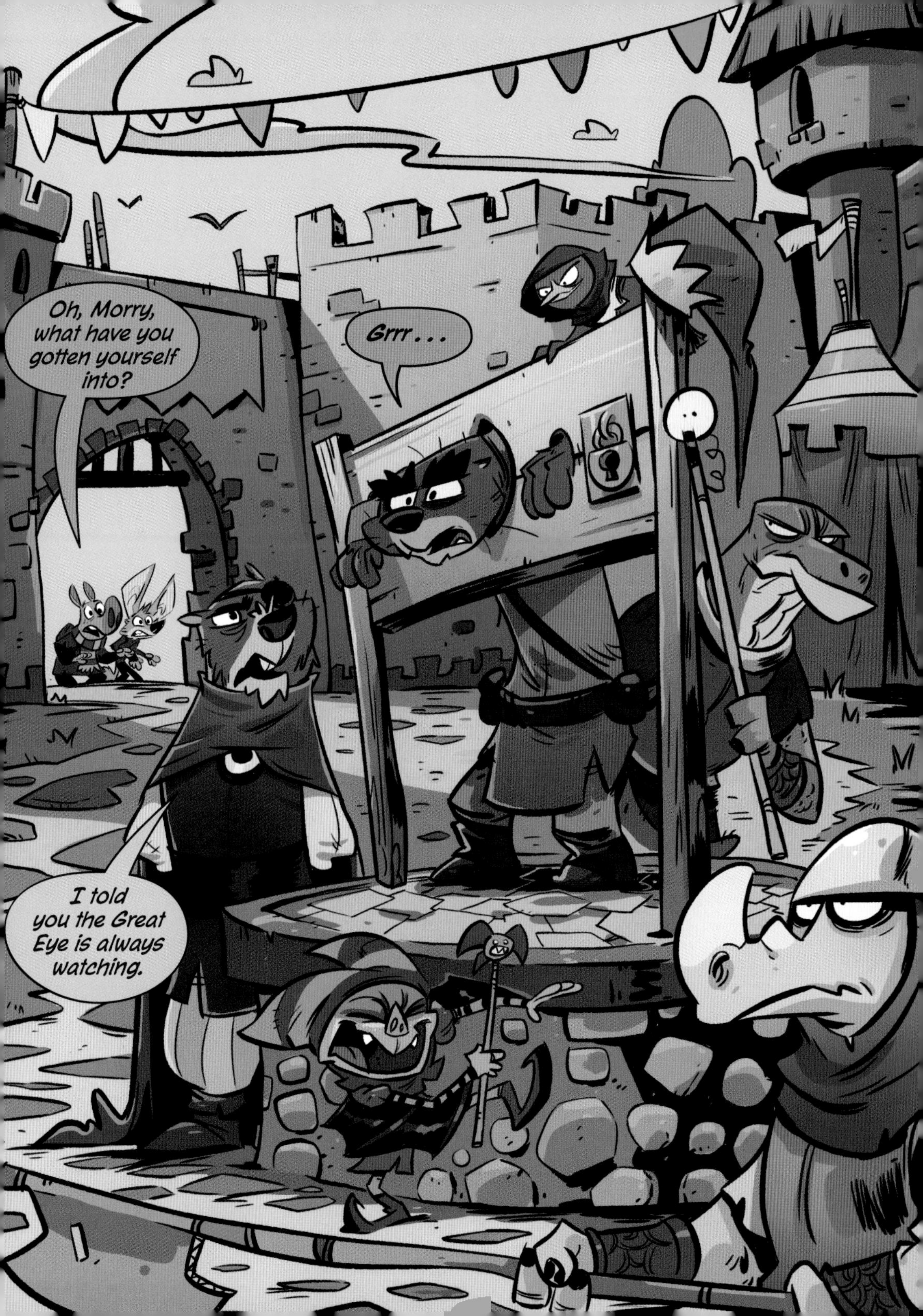
Oh, Morry, what have you gotten yourself into?
Grrr . . .
I told you the Great Eye is always watching.

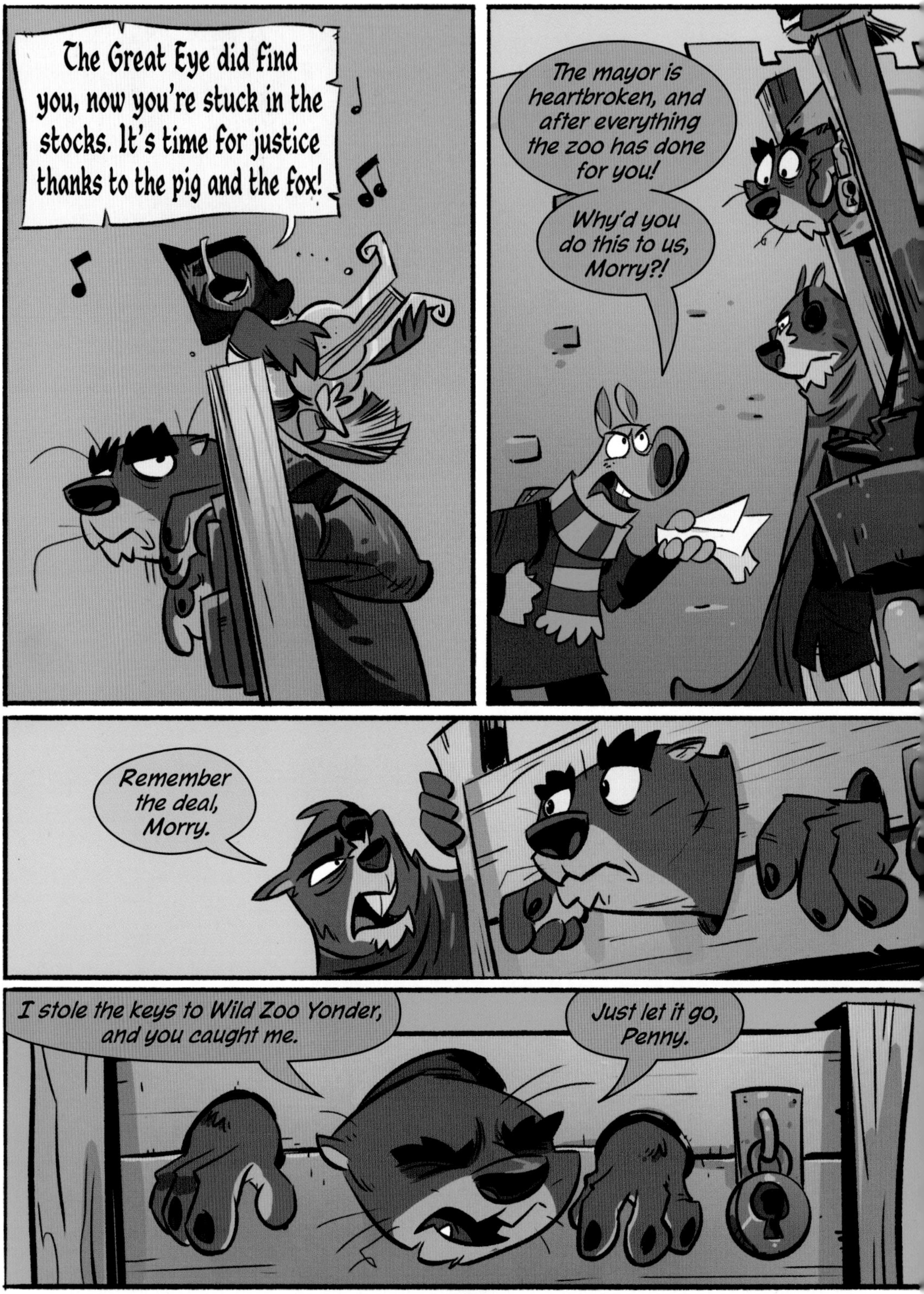
The Great Eye did find you, now you're stuck in the stocks. It's time for justice thanks to the pig and the fox!
The mayor is heartbroken, and after everything the zoo has done for you!
Why'd you do this to us, Morry?!
Remember the deal, Morry.
I stole the keys to Wild Zoo Yonder, and you caught me.
Just let it go, Penny.

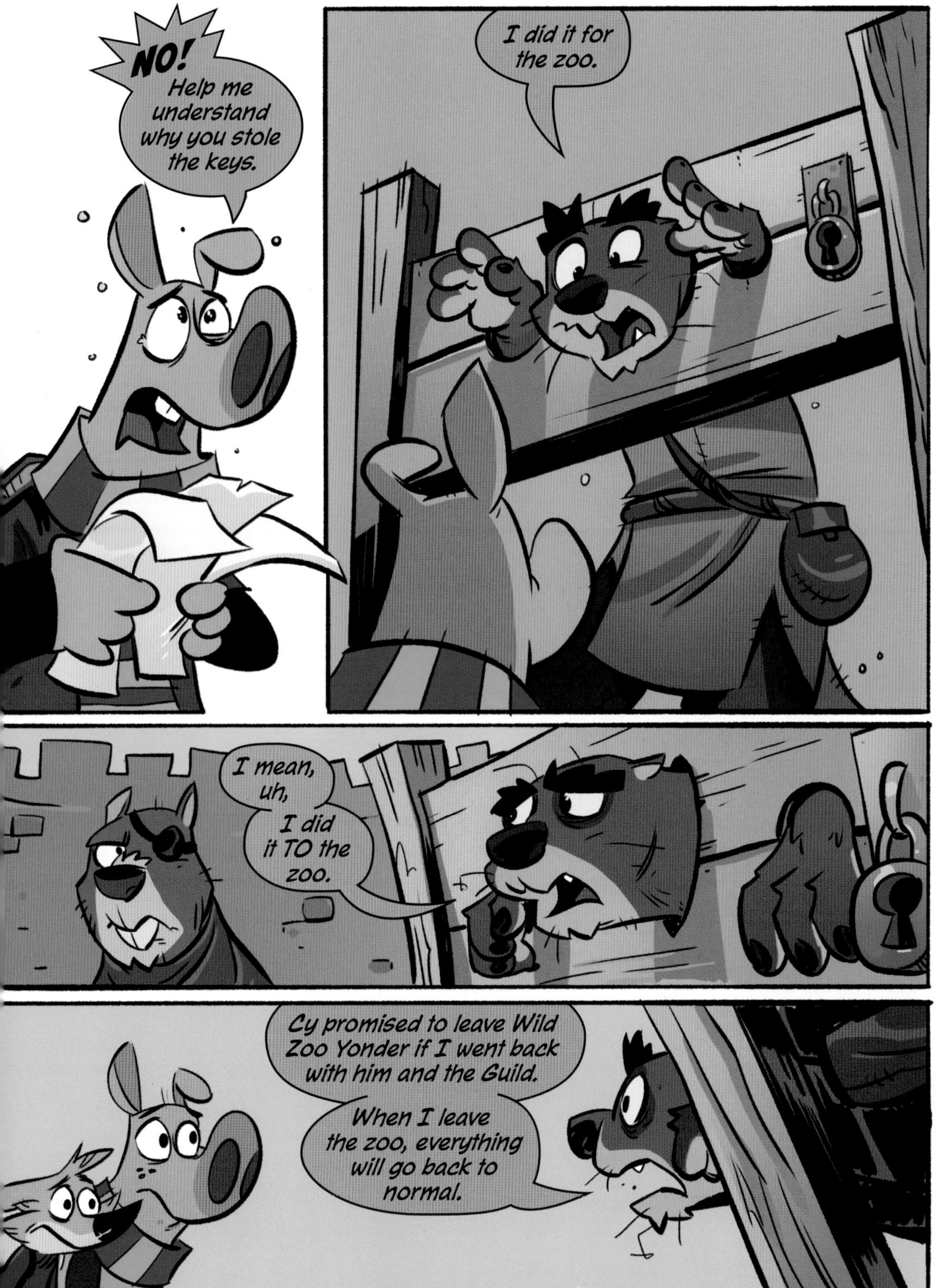
NO! Help me understand why you stole the keys.
I did it for the zoo.
I mean, uh,
I did it TO the zoo.
Cy promised to leave Wild Zoo Yonder if I went back with him and the Guild.
When I leave the zoo, everything will go back to normal.

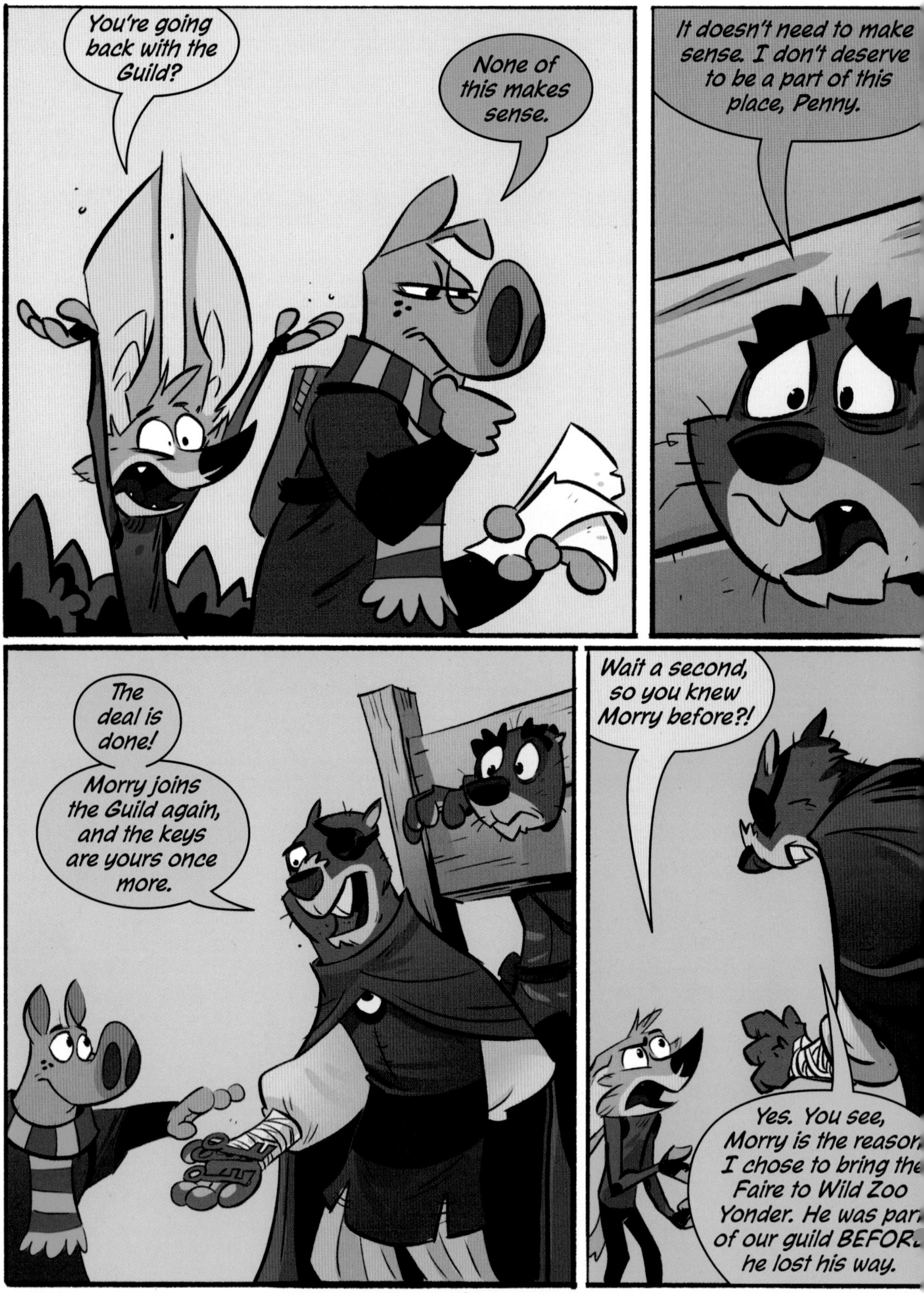

You're going back with the Guild?
None of this makes sense.
It doesn't need to make sense. I don't deserve to be a part of this place, Penny.
The deal is done!
Morry joins the Guild again, and the keys are yours once more.
Wait a second, so you knew Morry before?!
Yes. You see, Morry is the reason I chose to bring the Faire to Wild Zoo Yonder. He was part of our guild BEFORE he lost his way.

And once I learned he was here, I knew we had to come find him. But do not fret any longer; the Guild has their wizard again!

We must speak of happier times and worry no more.

Bring those keys to the mayor. She will keep them...

SAFE.

But we...

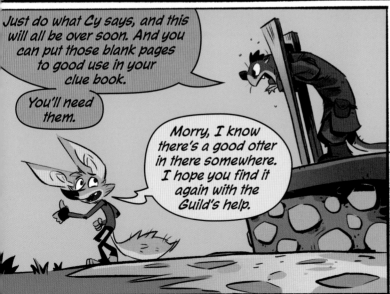

Just do what Cy says, and this will all be over soon. And you can put those blank pages to good use in your clue book.

You'll need them.

Morry, I know there's a good otter in there somewhere. I hope you find it again with the Guild's help.

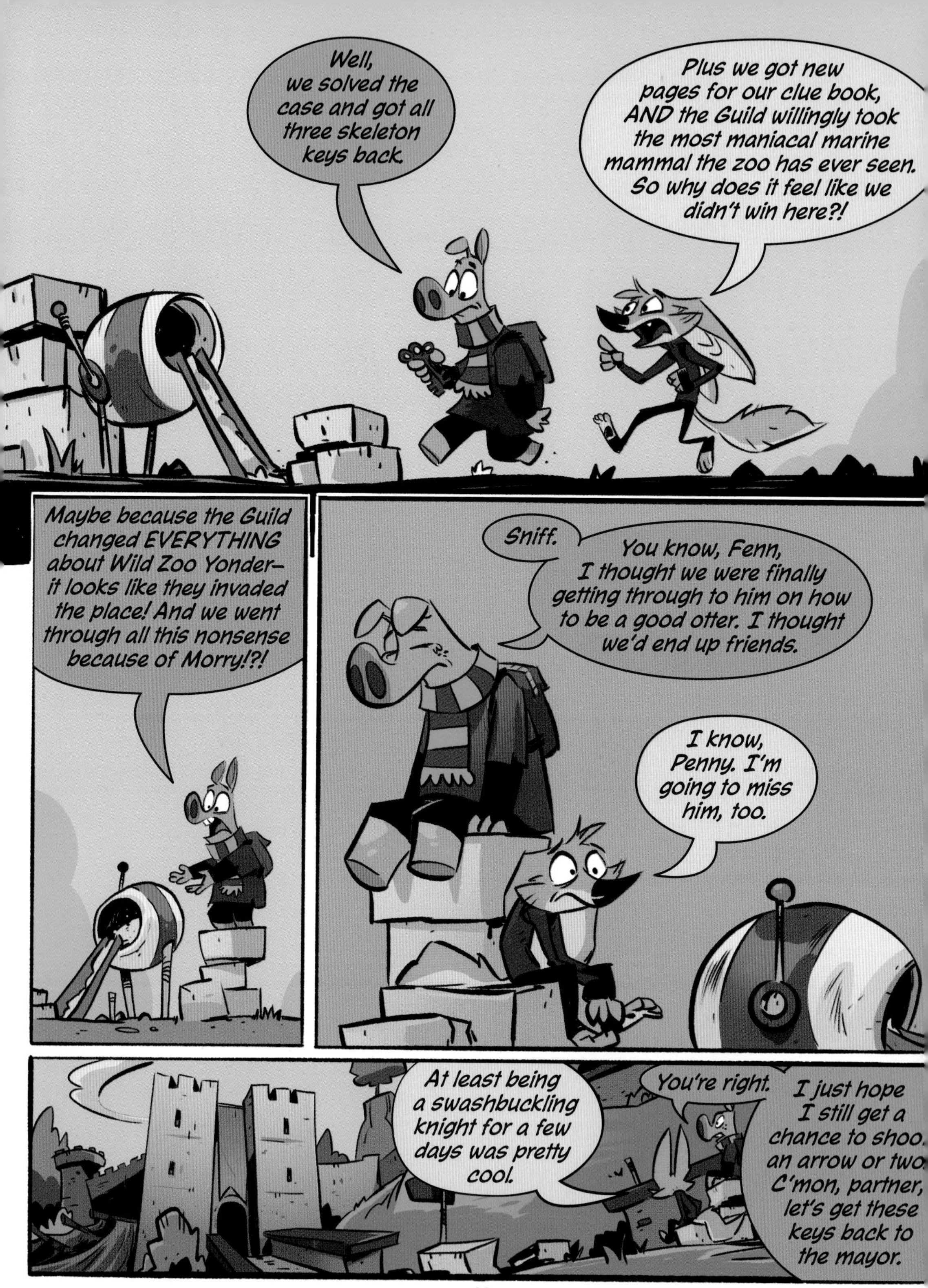

Well, we solved the case and got all three skeleton keys back.
Plus we got new pages for our clue book, AND the Guild willingly took the most maniacal marine mammal the zoo has ever seen. So why does it feel like we didn't win here?!
Maybe because the Guild changed EVERYTHING about Wild Zoo Yonder– it looks like they invaded the place! And we went through all this nonsense because of Morry!?!
Sniff.
You know, Fenn, I thought we were finally getting through to him on how to be a good otter. I thought we'd end up friends.
I know, Penny. I'm going to miss him, too.
At least being a swashbuckling knight for a few days was pretty cool.
You're right.
I just hope I still get a chance to shoo an arrow or two C'mon, partner, let's get these keys back to the mayor.

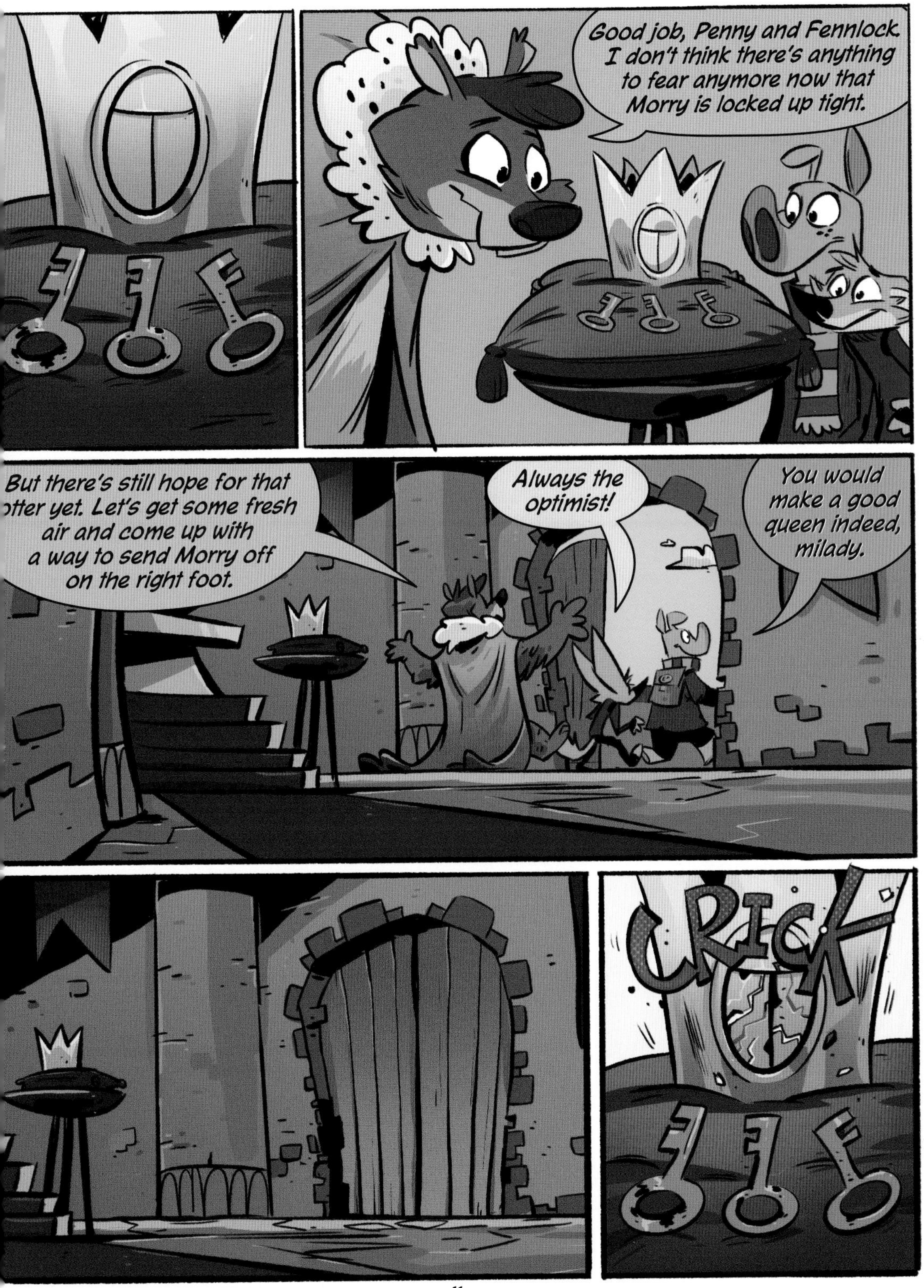
Good job, Penny and Fennlock. I don't think there's anything to fear anymore now that Morry is locked up tight.
But there's still hope for that otter yet. Let's get some fresh air and come up with a way to send Morry off on the right foot.
Always the optimist!
You would make a good queen indeed, milady.
CRICK!

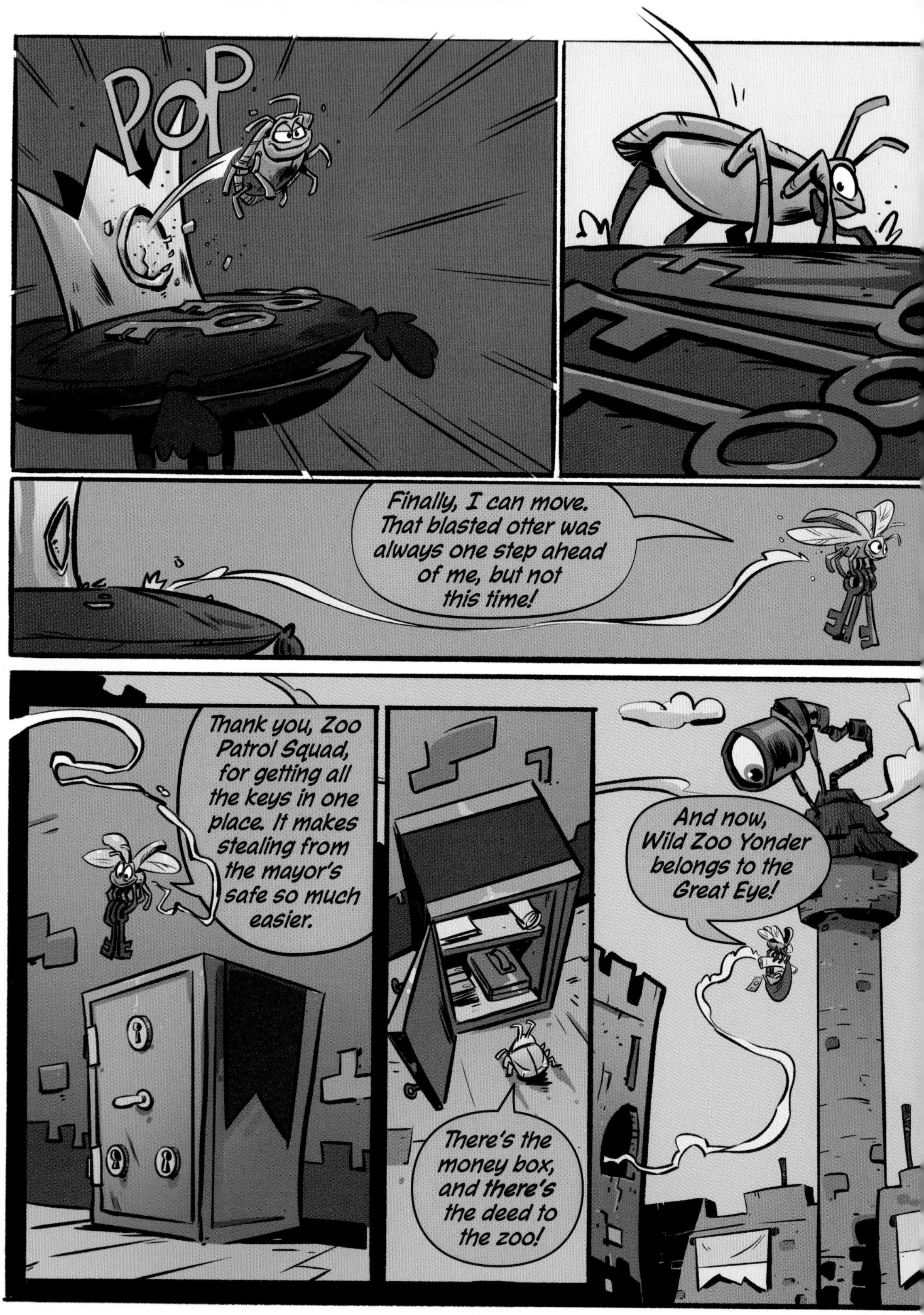
POP
Finally, I can move. That blasted otter was always one step ahead of me, but not this time!
Thank you, Zoo Patrol Squad, for getting all the keys in one place. It makes stealing from the mayor's safe so much easier.
There's the money box, and there's the deed to the zoo!
And now, Wild Zoo Yonder belongs to the Great Eye!

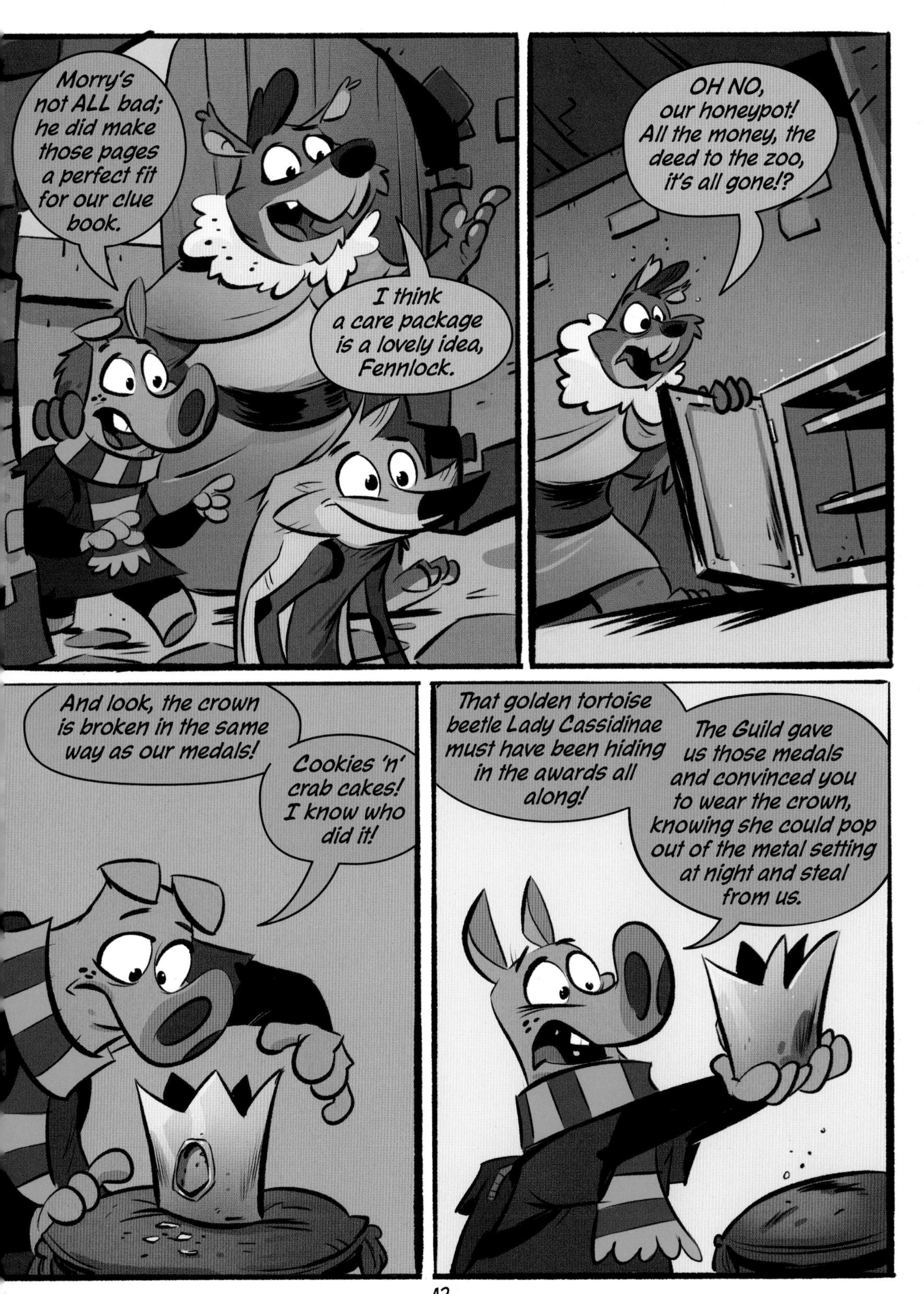
Morry's not ALL bad; he did make those pages a perfect fit for our clue book.
I think a care package is a lovely idea, Fennlock.
OH NO, our honeypot! All the money, the deed to the zoo, it's all gone!?
And look, the crown is broken in the same way as our medals!
Cookies 'n' crab cakes! I know who did it!
That golden tortoise beetle Lady Cassidinae must have been hiding in the awards all along!
The Guild gave us those medals and convinced you to wear the crown, knowing she could pop out of the metal setting at night and steal from us.

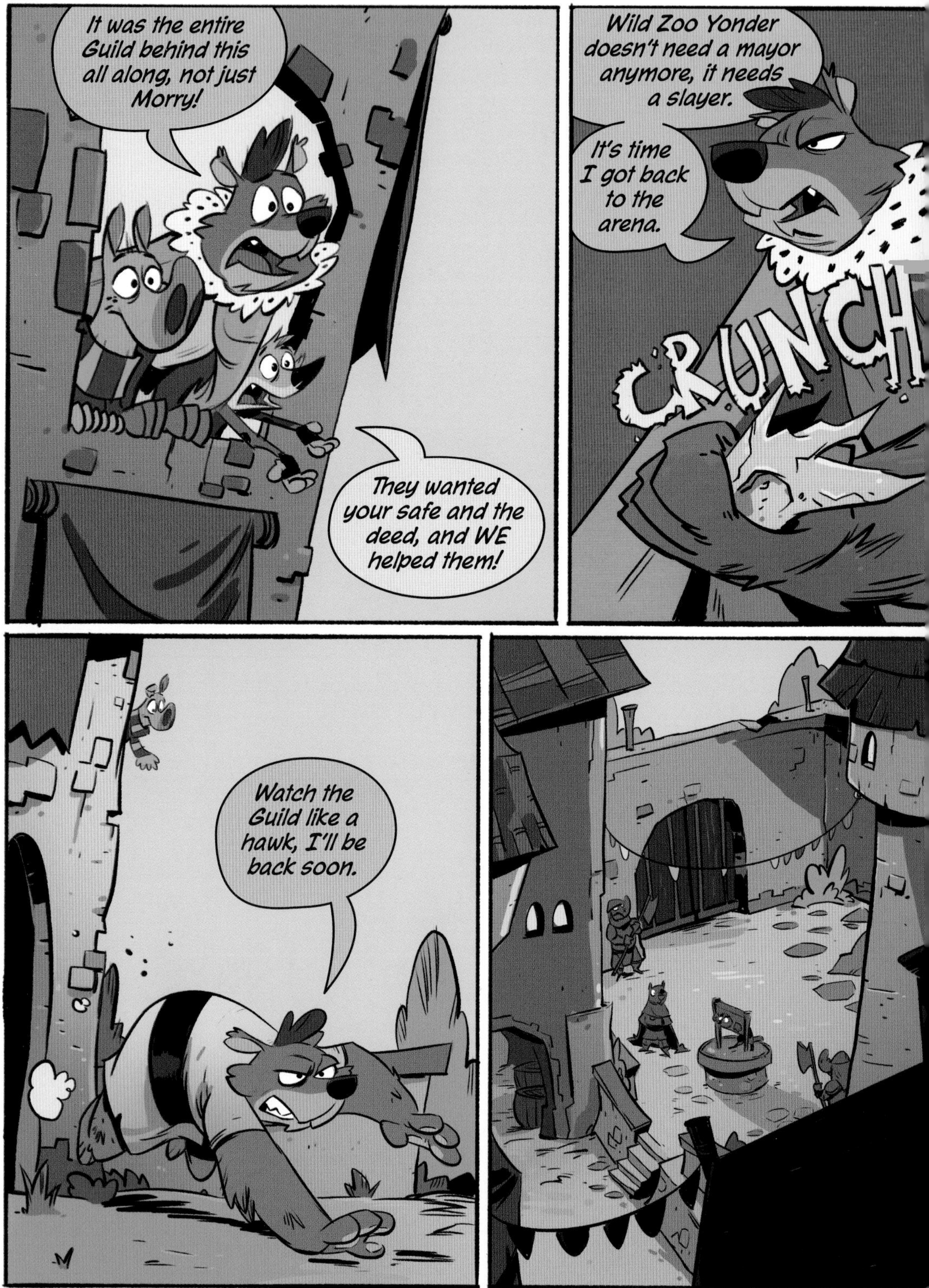
It was the entire Guild behind this all along, not just Morry!
They wanted your safe and the deed, and WE helped them!
Wild Zoo Yonder doesn't need a mayor anymore, it needs a slayer.
It's time I got back to the arena.
CRUNCH
Watch the Guild like a hawk, I'll be back soon.

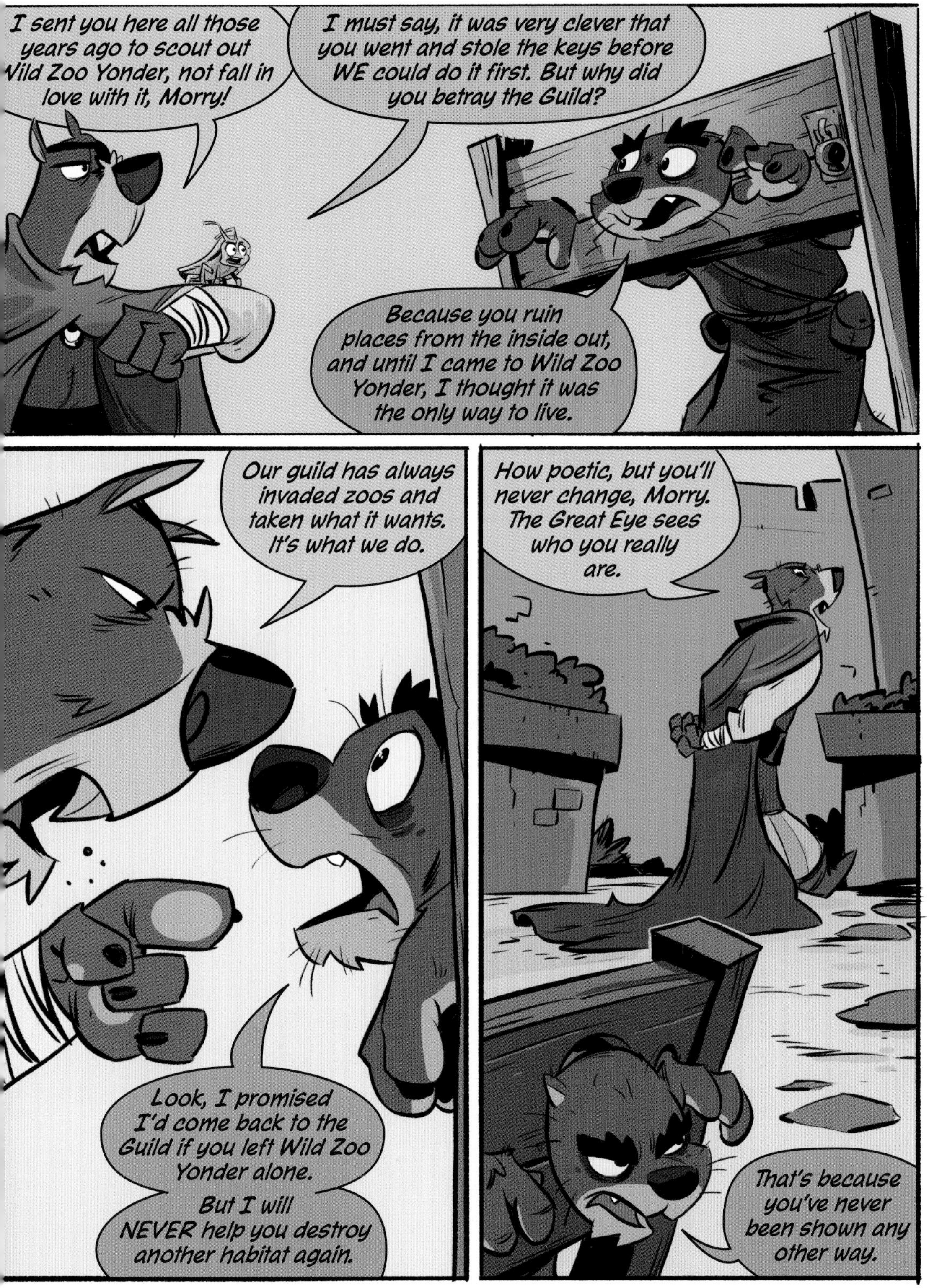
I sent you here all those years ago to scout out Wild Zoo Yonder, not fall in love with it, Morry!
I must say, it was very clever that you went and stole the keys before WE could do it first. But why did you betray the Guild?
Because you ruin places from the inside out, and until I came to Wild Zoo Yonder, I thought it was the only way to live.
Our guild has always invaded zoos and taken what it wants. It's what we do.
Look, I promised I'd come back to the Guild if you left Wild Zoo Yonder alone.
But I will NEVER help you destroy another habitat again.
How poetic, but you'll never change, Morry. The Great Eye sees who you really are.
That's because you've never been shown any other way.

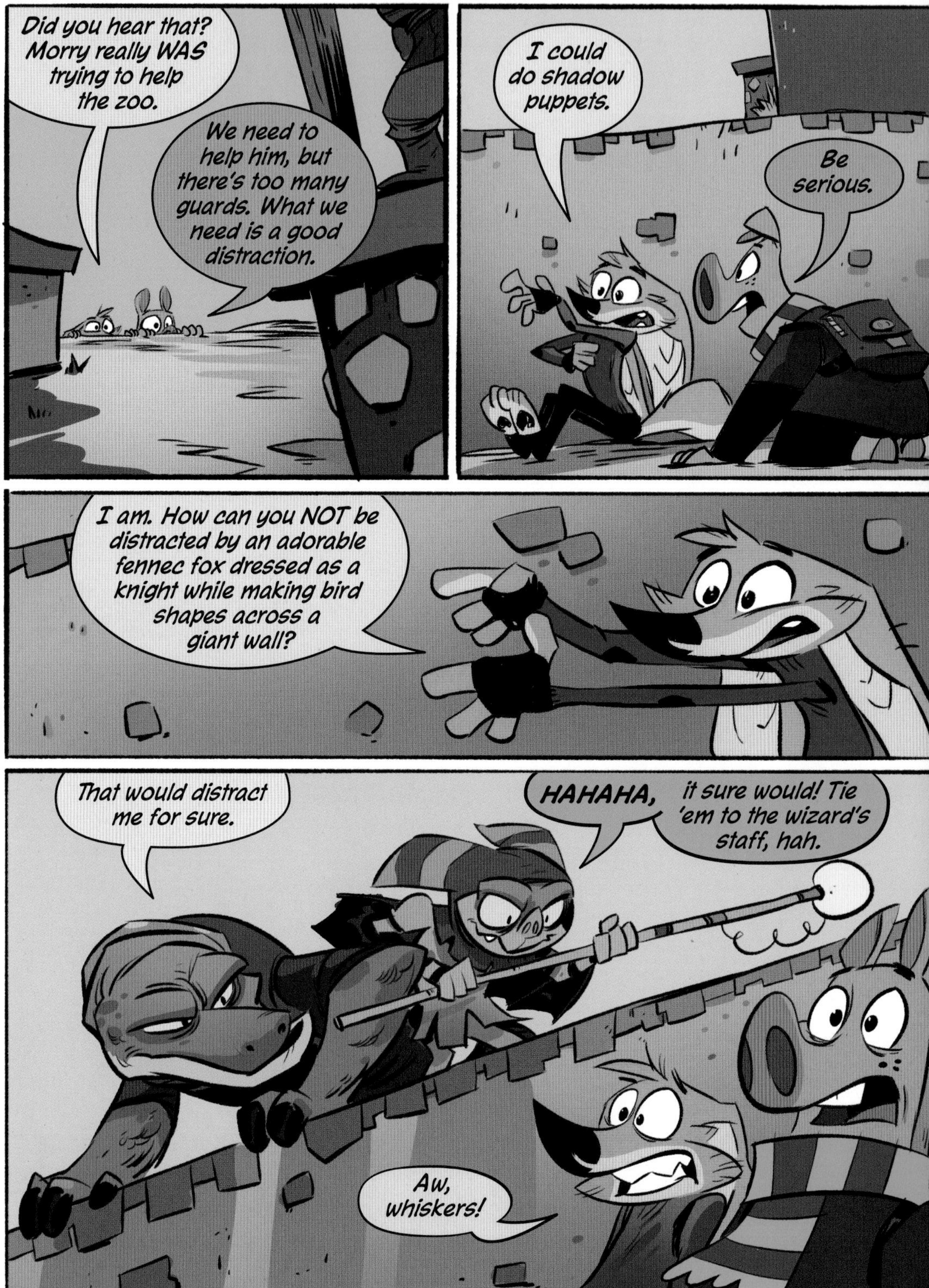
Did you hear that? Morry really WAS trying to help the zoo.
We need to help him, but there's too many guards. What we need is a good distraction.
I could do shadow puppets.
Be serious.
I am. How can you NOT be distracted by an adorable fennec fox dressed as a knight while making bird shapes across a giant wall?
That would distract me for sure.
HAHAHA,
it sure would! Tie 'em to the wizard's staff, hah.
Aw, whiskers!

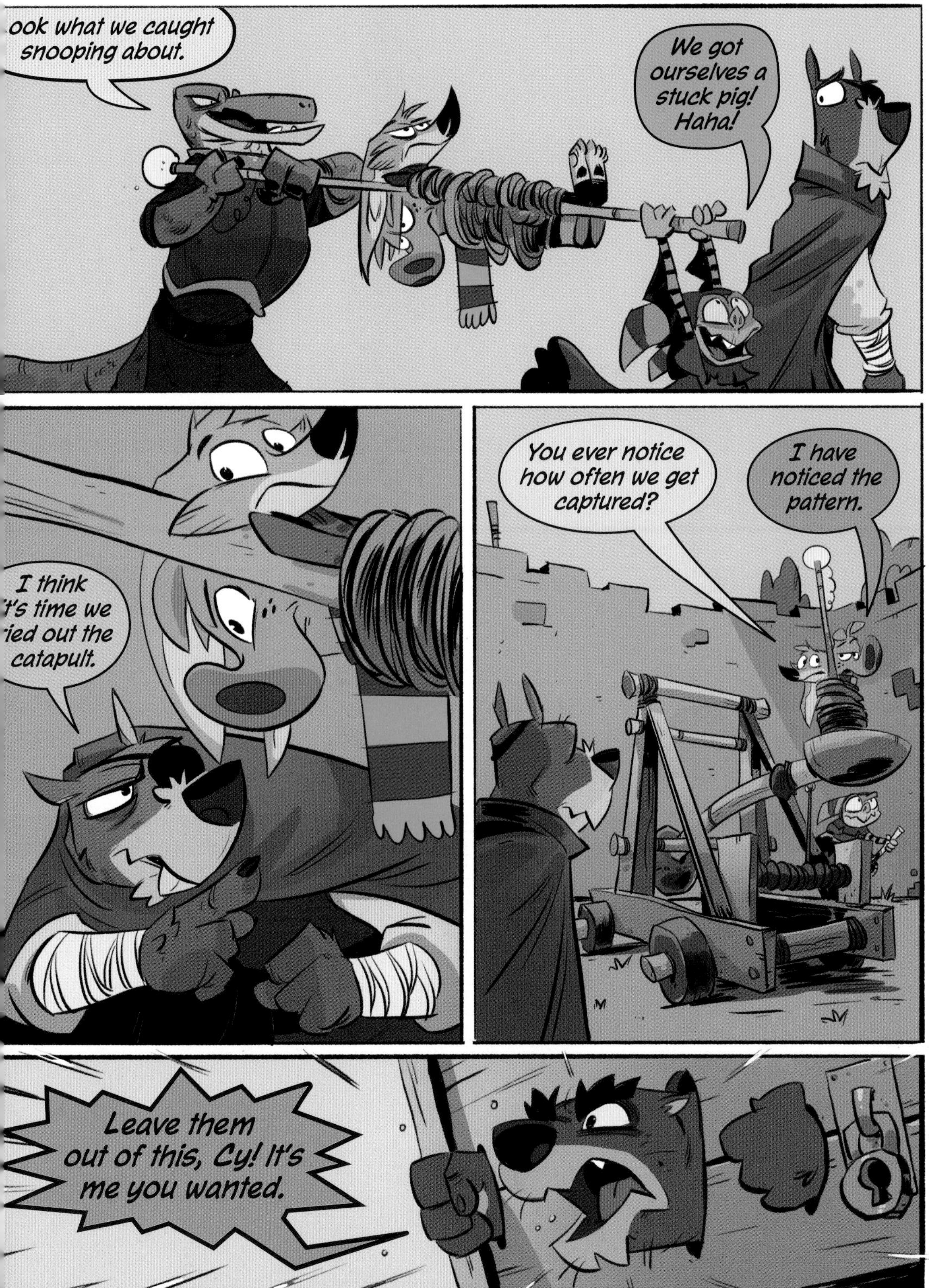
ook what we caught snooping about.
We got ourselves a stuck pig! Haha!
I think 't's time we ied out the catapult.
You ever notice how often we get captured?
I have noticed the pattern.
Leave them out of this, Cy! It's me you wanted.

He lied, Morry. Lady Cassidinae broke into the safe, and the Guild took everything.

They were never going to let the zoo go.

But you promised to leave the zoo alone.

What can I say, I'm an invasive species, and invading is what I do best.

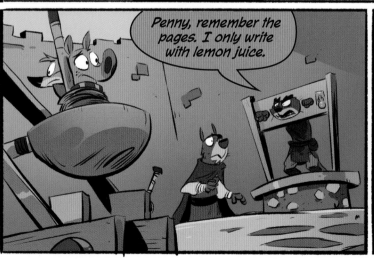

Penny, remember the pages. I only write with lemon juice.

FLFF

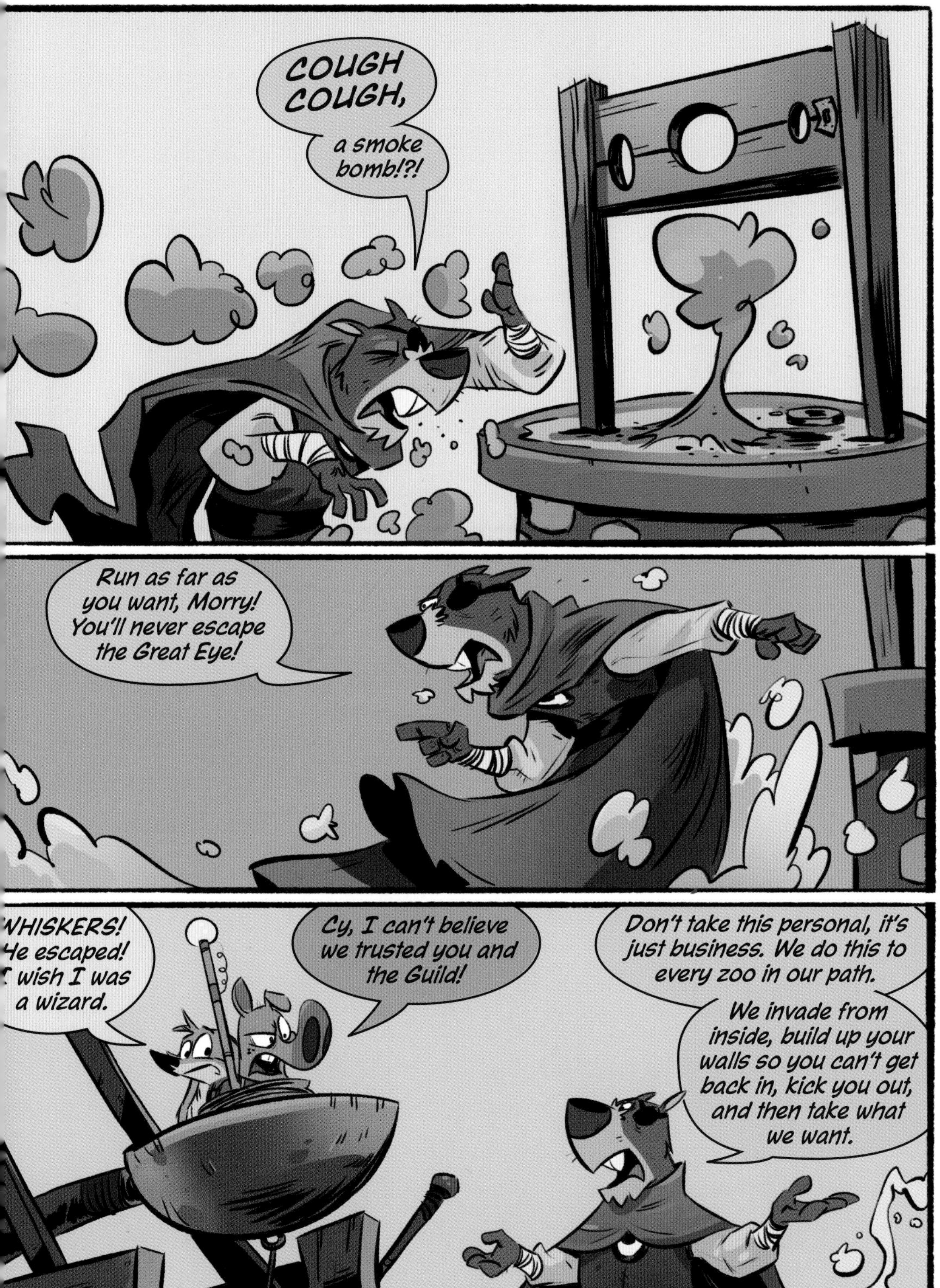
COUGH COUGH,
a smoke bomb!?!
Run as far as you want, Morry! You'll never escape the Great Eye!
WHISKERS! He escaped! I wish I was a wizard.
Cy, I can't believe we trusted you and the Guild!
Don't take this personal, it's just business. We do this to every zoo in our path.
We invade from inside, build up your walls so you can't get back in, kick you out, and then take what we want.

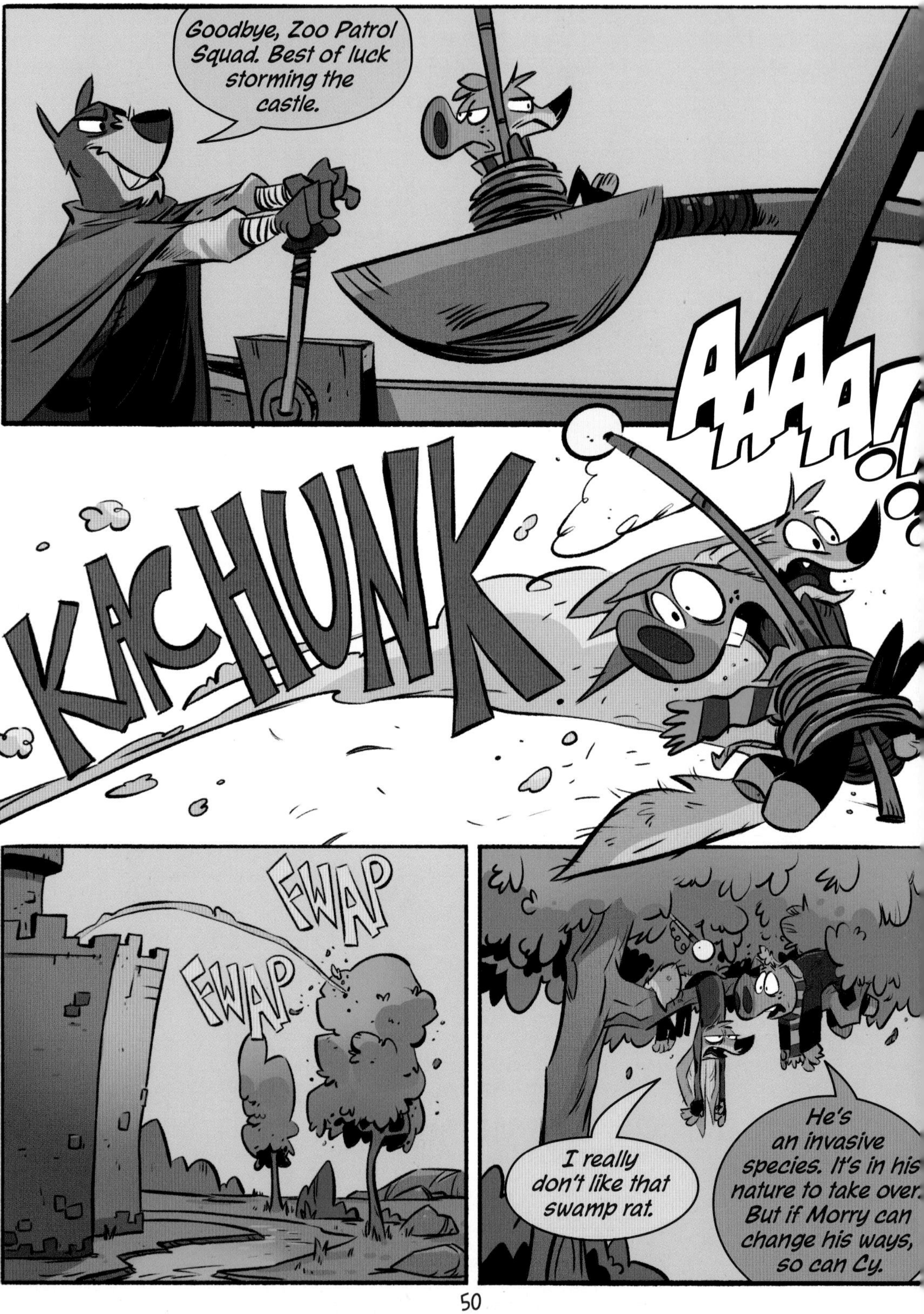

Goodbye, Zoo Patrol Squad. Best of luck storming the castle.
AAAA
KACHUNK
FWAP
FWAP
I really don't like that swamp rat.
He's an invasive species. It's in his nature to take over. But if Morry can change his ways, so can Cy.

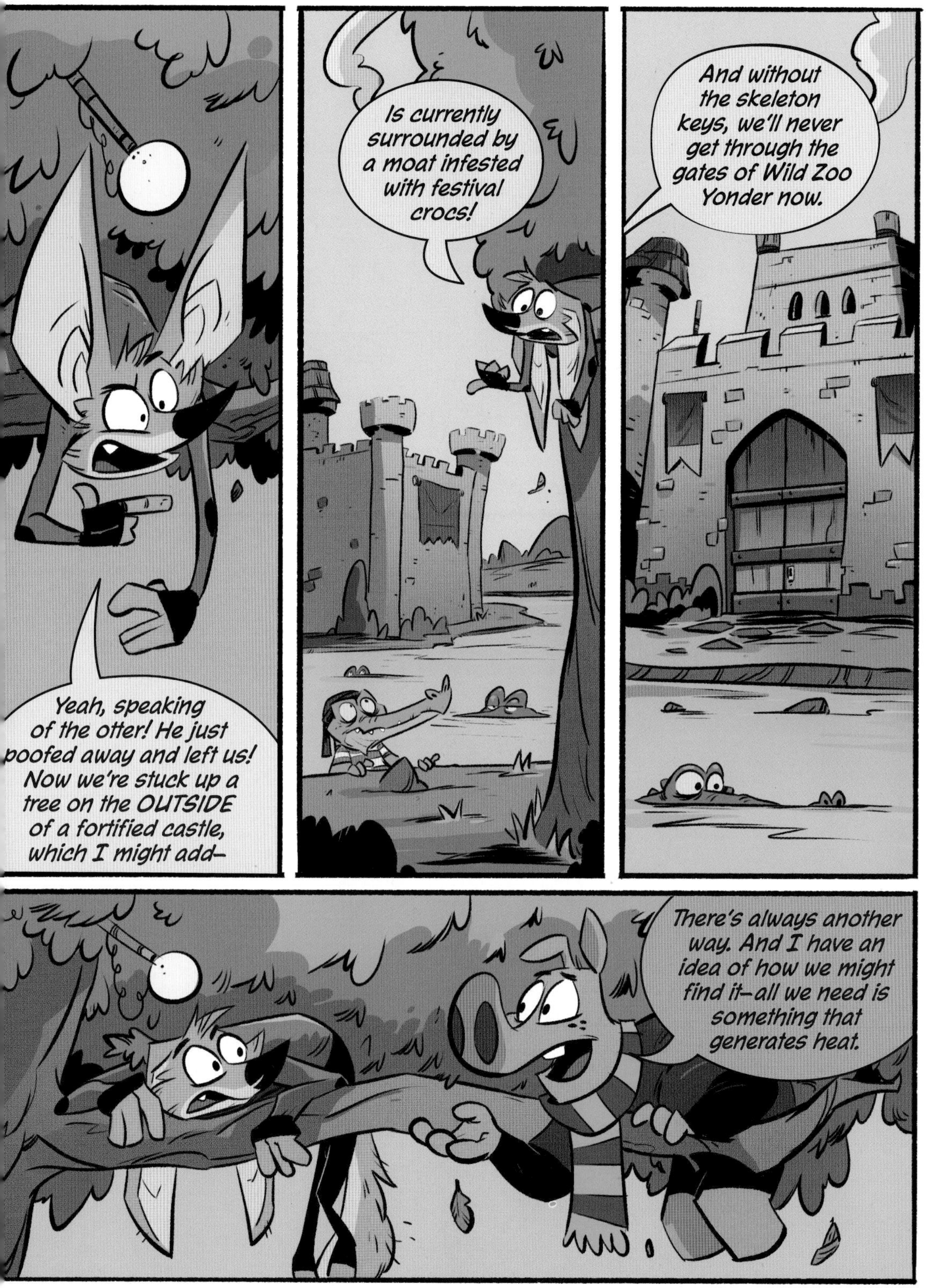

Yeah, speaking of the otter! He just poofed away and left us! Now we're stuck up a tree on the OUTSIDE of a fortified castle, which I might add—
Is currently surrounded by a moat infested with festival crocs!
And without the skeleton keys, we'll never get through the gates of Wild Zoo Yonder now.
There's always another way. And I have an idea of how we might find it—all we need is something that generates heat.

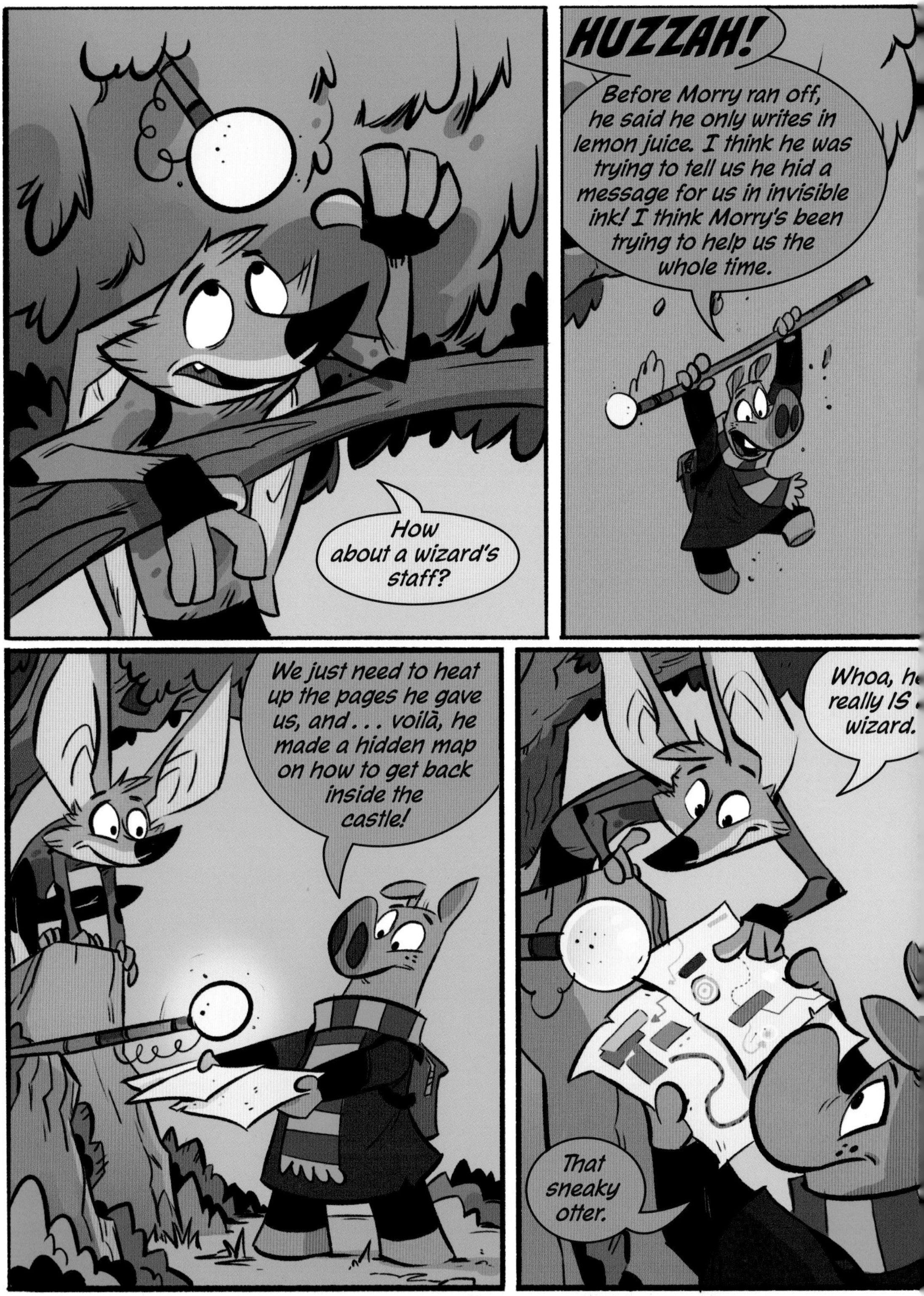
How about a wizard's staff?
HUZZAH!
Before Morry ran off, he said he only writes in lemon juice. I think he was trying to tell us he hid a message for us in invisible ink! I think Morry's been trying to help us the whole time.
We just need to heat up the pages he gave us, and . . . voilà, he made a hidden map on how to get back inside the castle!
Whoa, he really IS a wizard.
That sneaky otter.

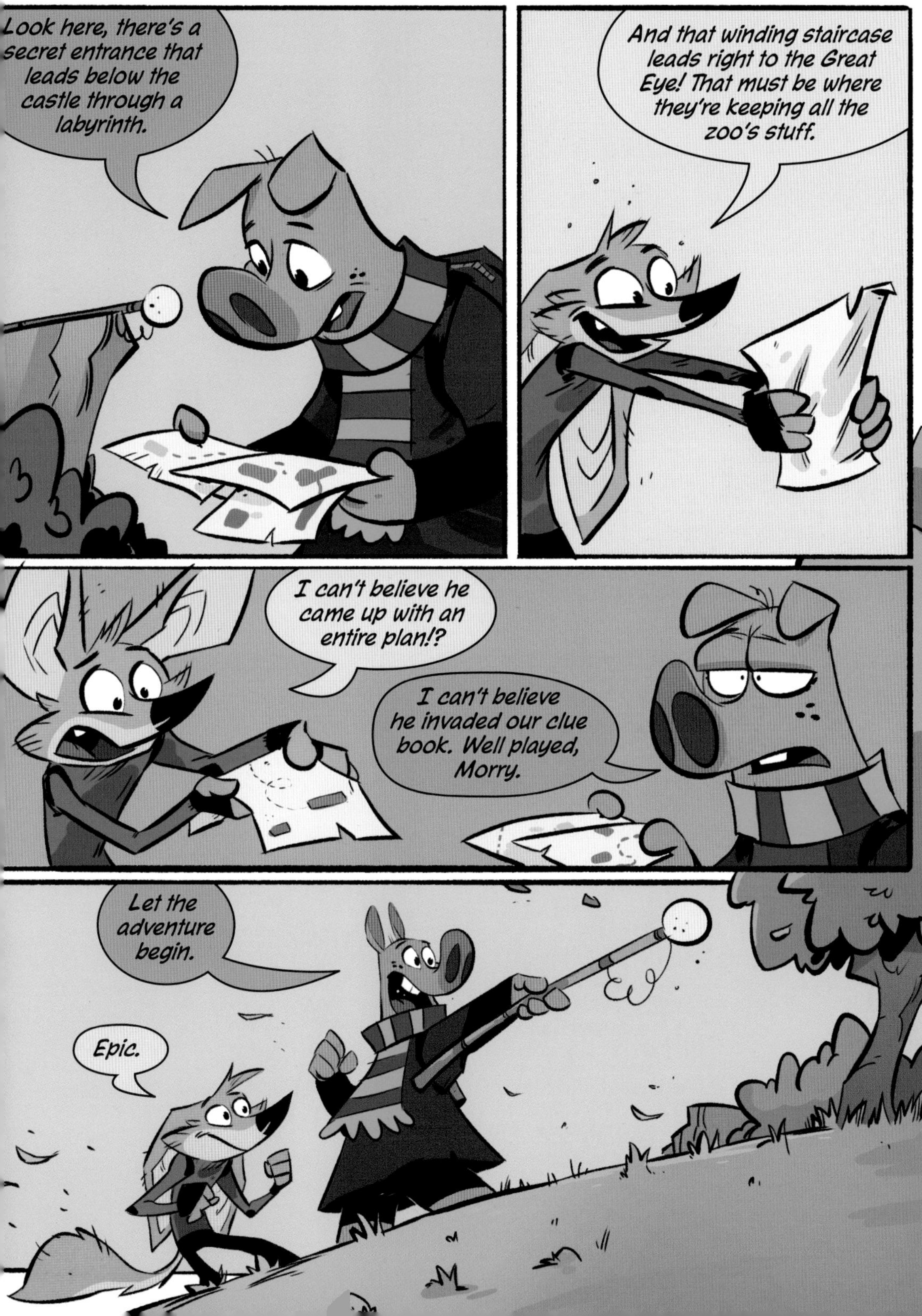
Look here, there's a secret entrance that leads below the castle through a labyrinth.
And that winding staircase leads right to the Great Eye! That must be where they're keeping all the zoo's stuff.
I can't believe he came up with an entire plan!?
I can't believe he invaded our clue book. Well played, Morry.
Let the adventure begin.
Epic.

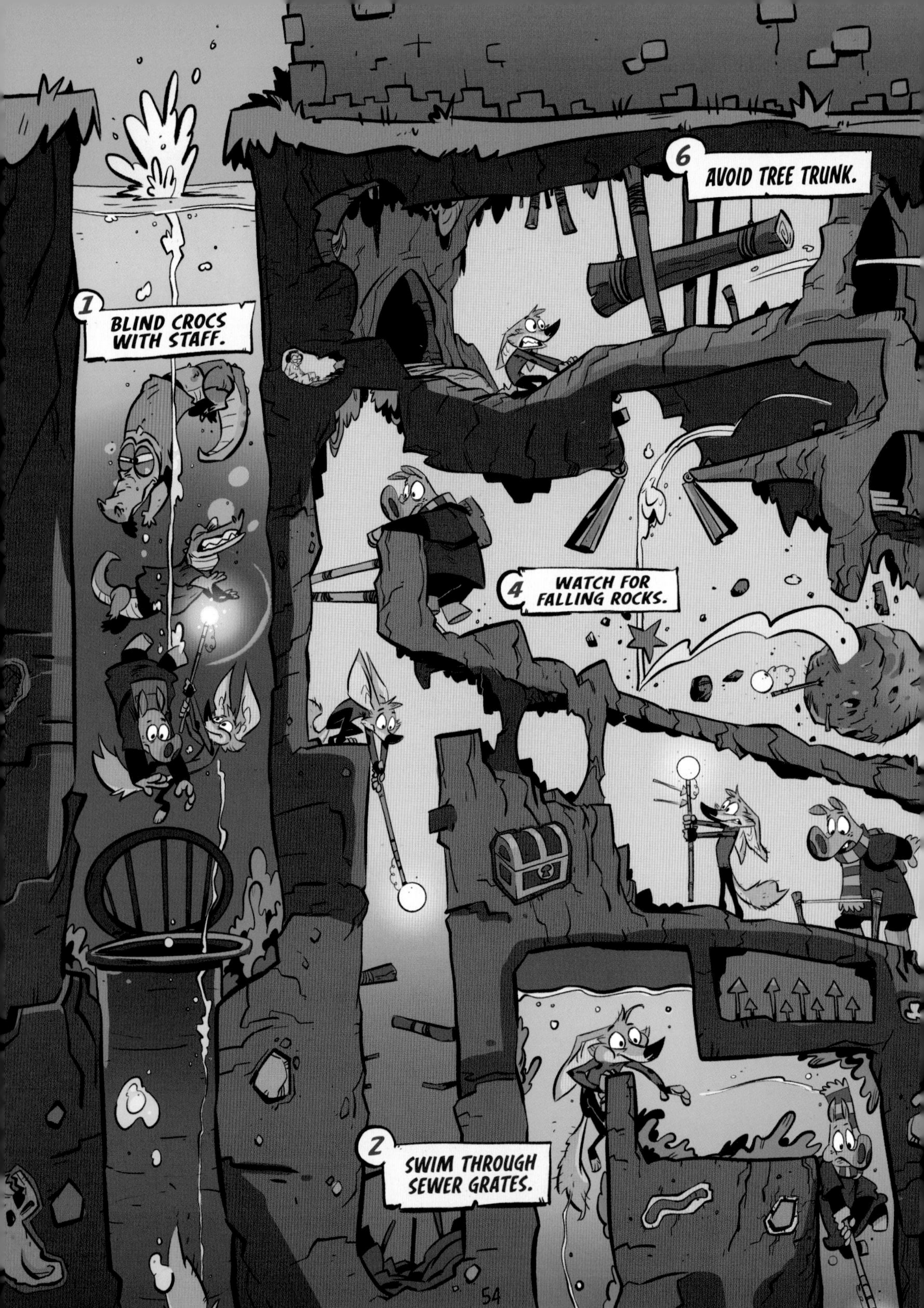
6 AVOID TREE TRUNK.
1 BLIND CROCS WITH STAFF.
4 WATCH FOR FALLING ROCKS.
2 SWIM THROUGH SEWER GRATES.

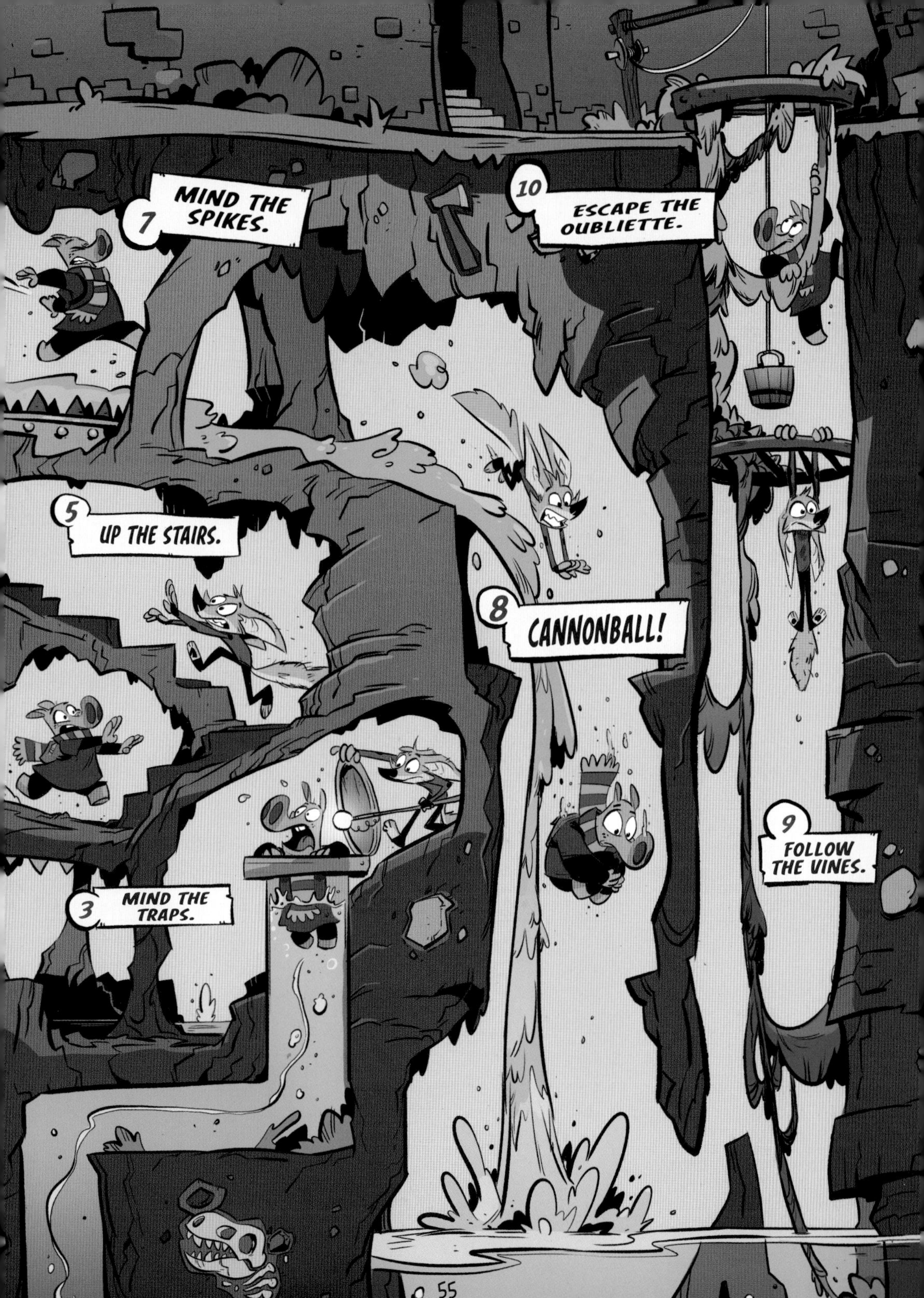

7 MIND THE SPIKES.
10 ESCAPE THE OUBLIETTE.
5 UP THE STAIRS.
8 CANNONBALL!
9 FOLLOW THE VINES.
3 MIND THE TRAPS.

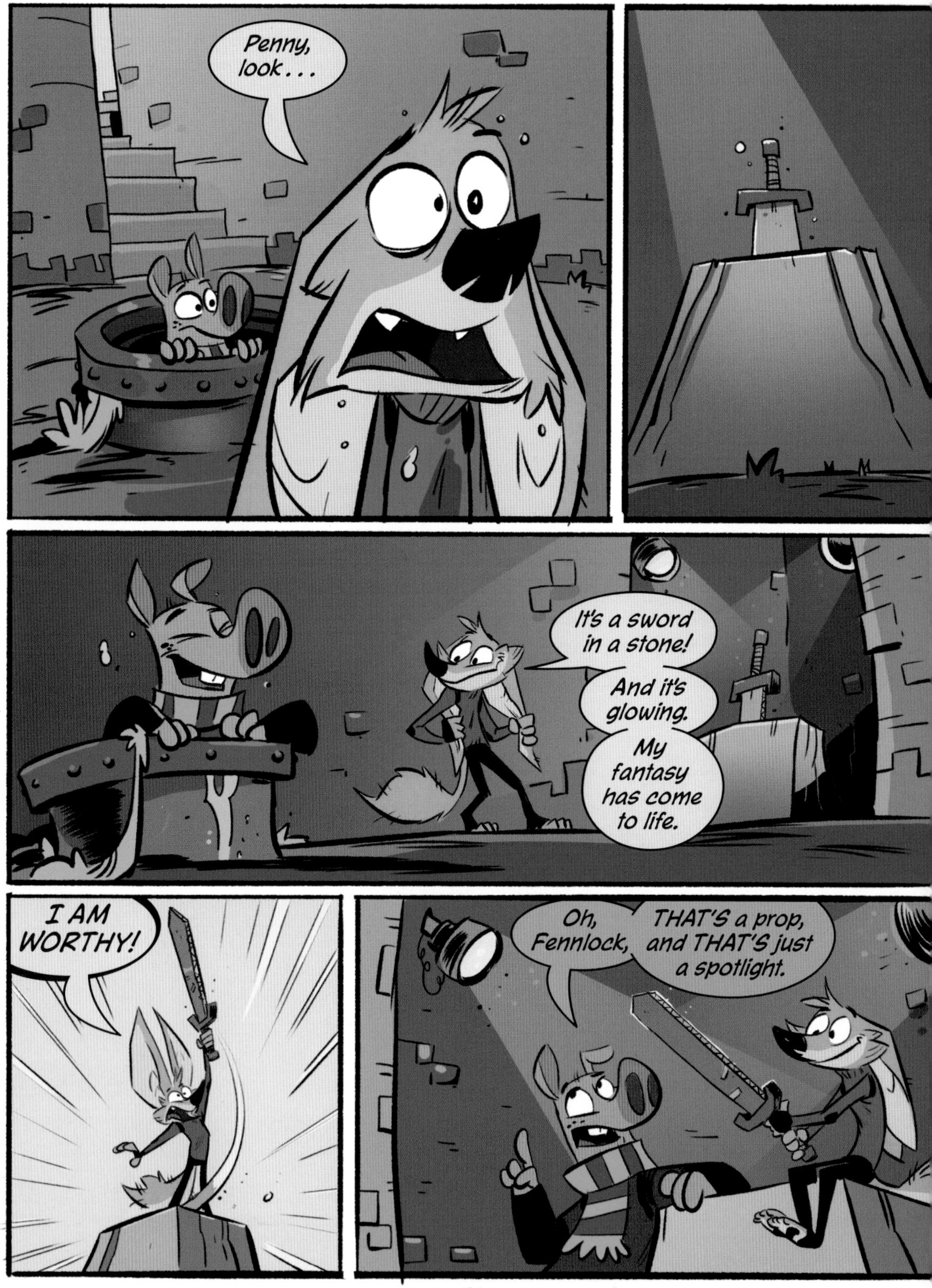
Penny, look . . .
It's a sword in a stone!
And it's glowing.
My fantasy has come to life.
I AM WORTHY!
Oh, Fennlock,
THAT'S a prop, and THAT'S just a spotlight.

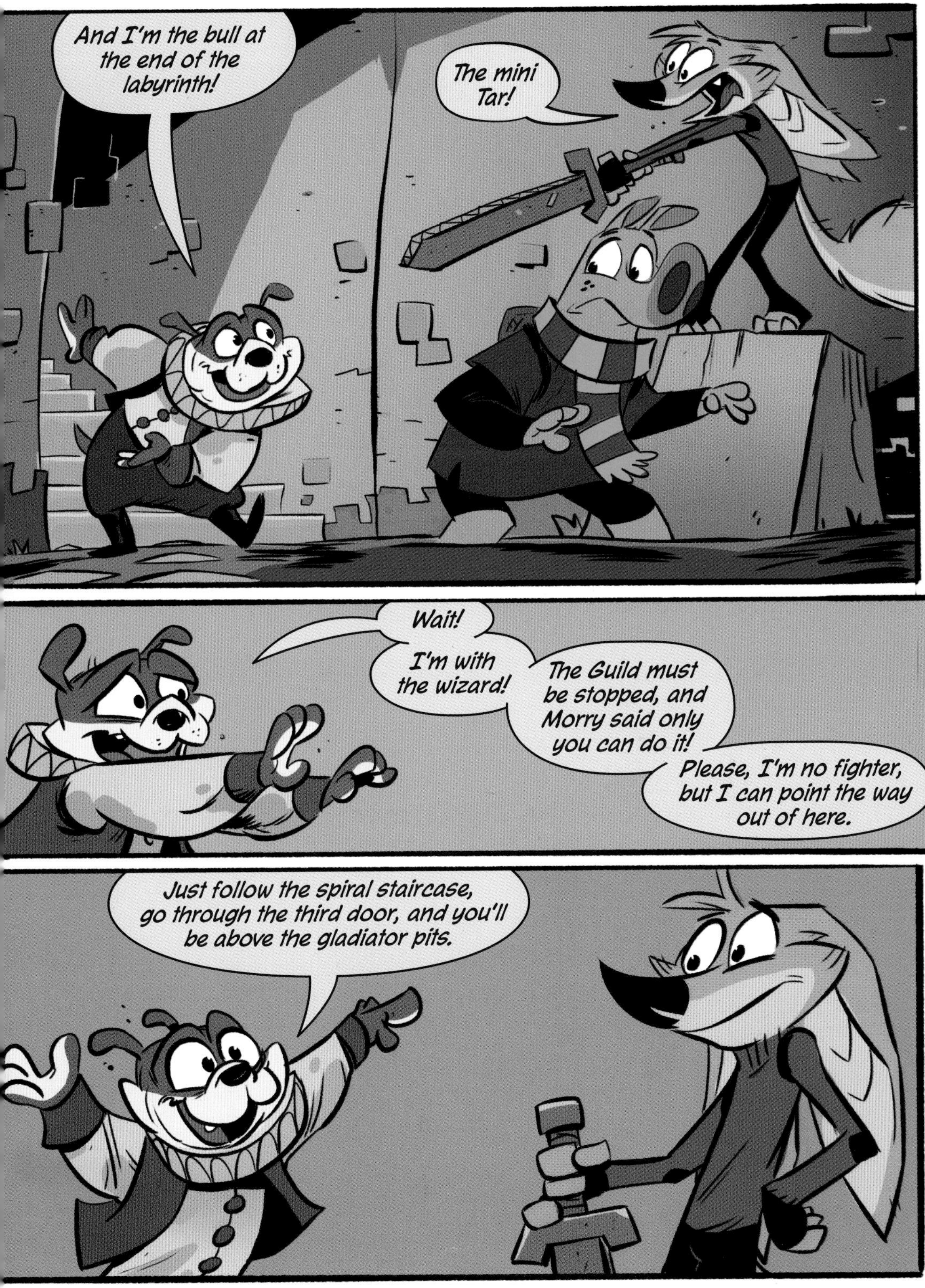
And I'm the bull at the end of the labyrinth!
The mini Tar!
Wait!
I'm with the wizard!
The Guild must be stopped, and Morry said only you can do it!
Please, I'm no fighter, but I can point the way out of here.
Just follow the spiral staircase, go through the third door, and you'll be above the gladiator pits.

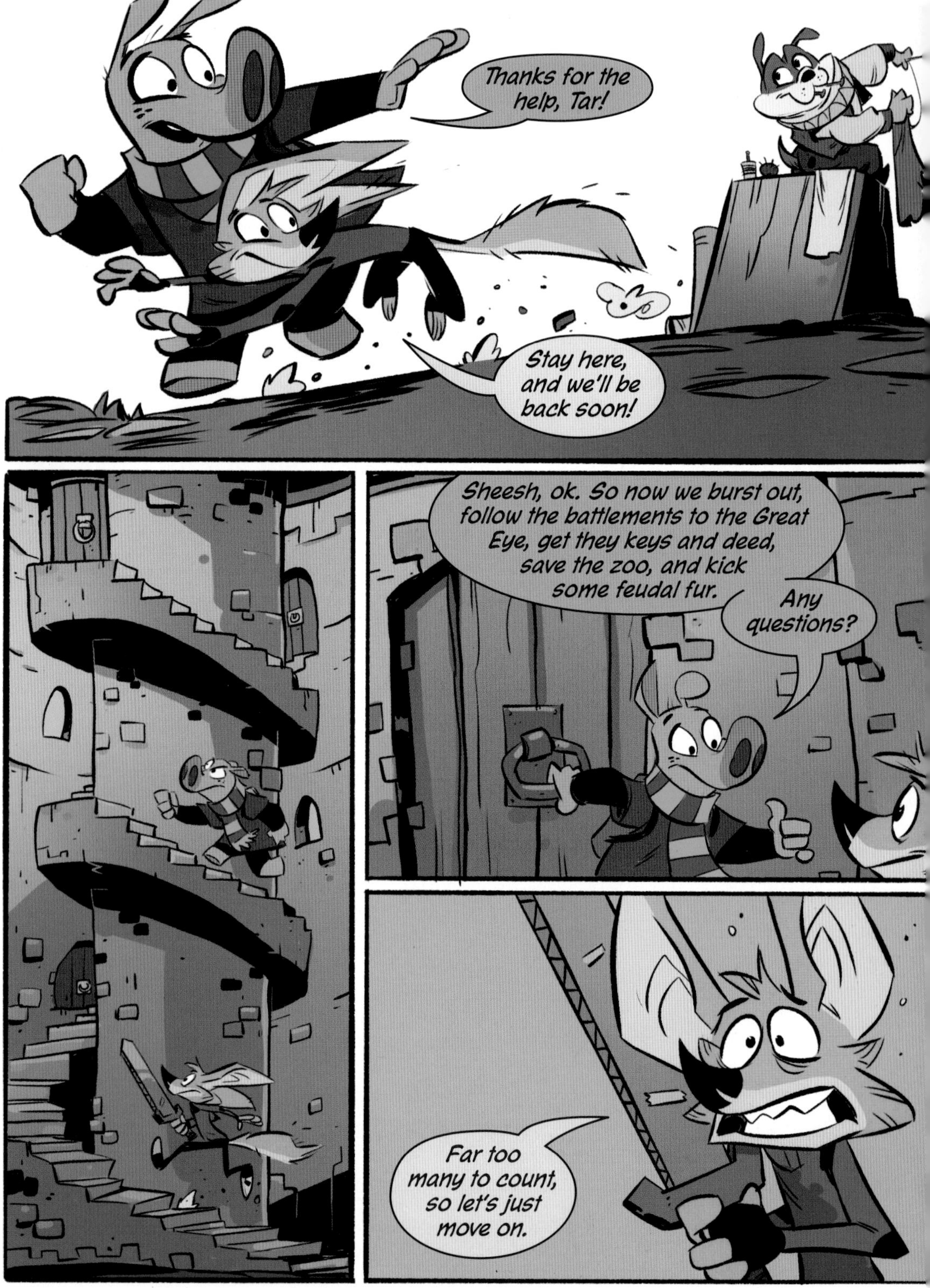
Thanks for the help, Tar!
Stay here, and we'll be back soon!
Sheesh, ok. So now we burst out, follow the battlements to the Great Eye, get they keys and deed, save the zoo, and kick some feudal fur.
Any questions?
Far too many to count, so let's just move on.

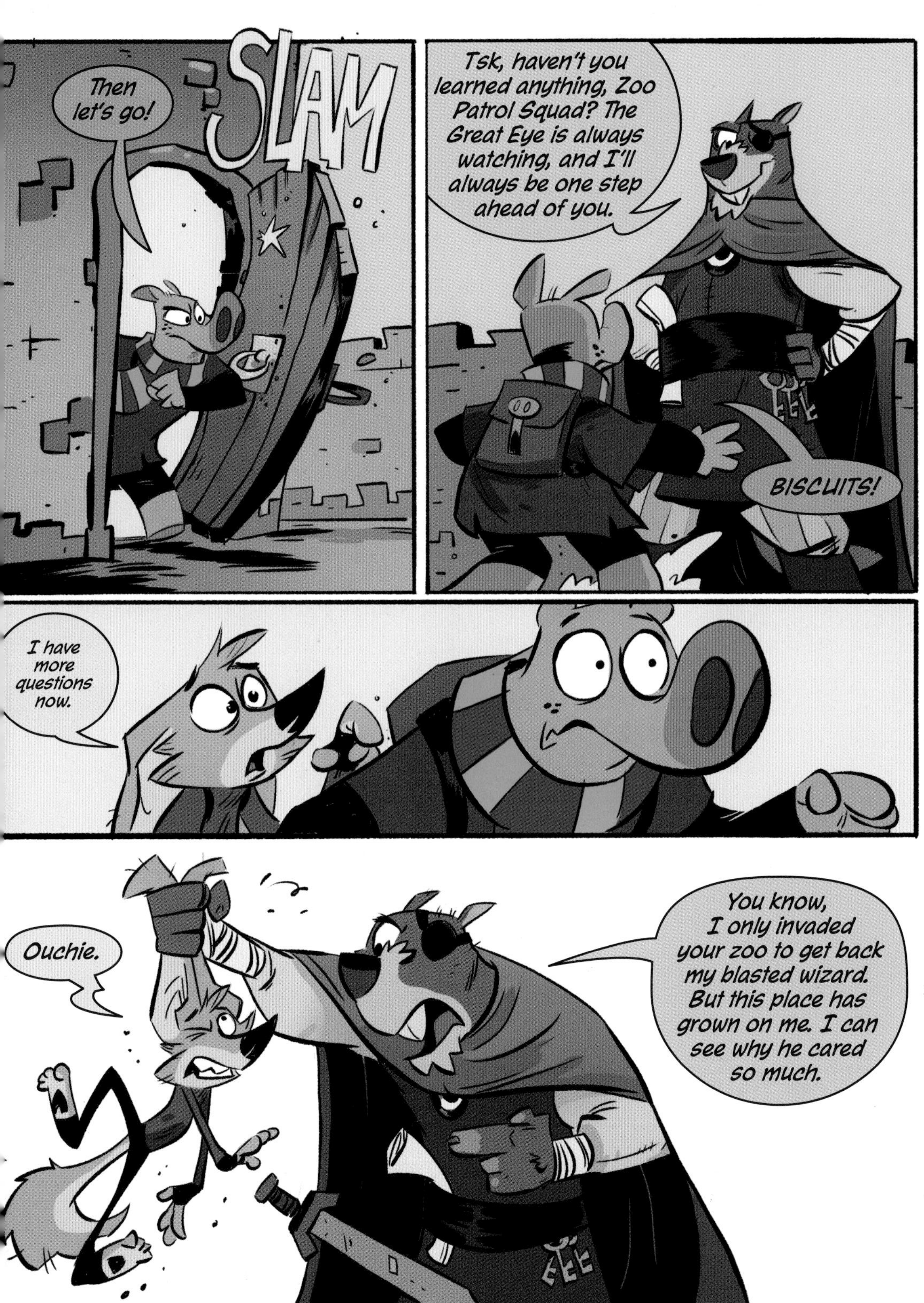
Then let's go!
SLAM
Tsk, haven't you learned anything, Zoo Patrol Squad? The Great Eye is always watching, and I'll always be one step ahead of you.
BISCUITS!
I have more questions now.
Ouchie.
You know, I only invaded your zoo to get back my blasted wizard. But this place has grown on me. I can see why he cared so much.

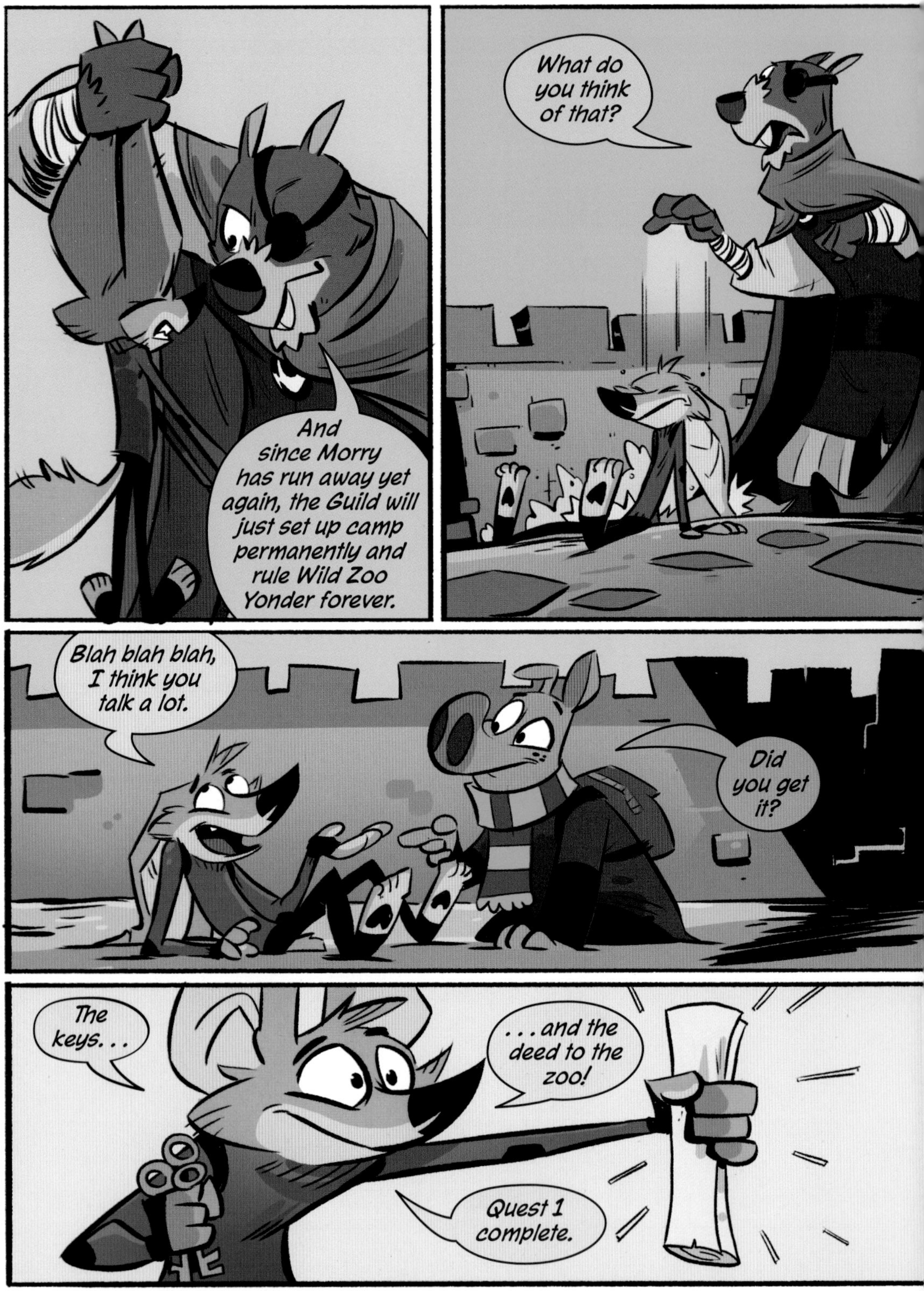
And since Morry has run away yet again, the Guild will just set up camp permanently and rule Wild Zoo Yonder forever.
What do you think of that?
Blah blah blah, I think you talk a lot.
Did you get it?
The keys...
...and the deed to the zoo!
Quest 1 complete.

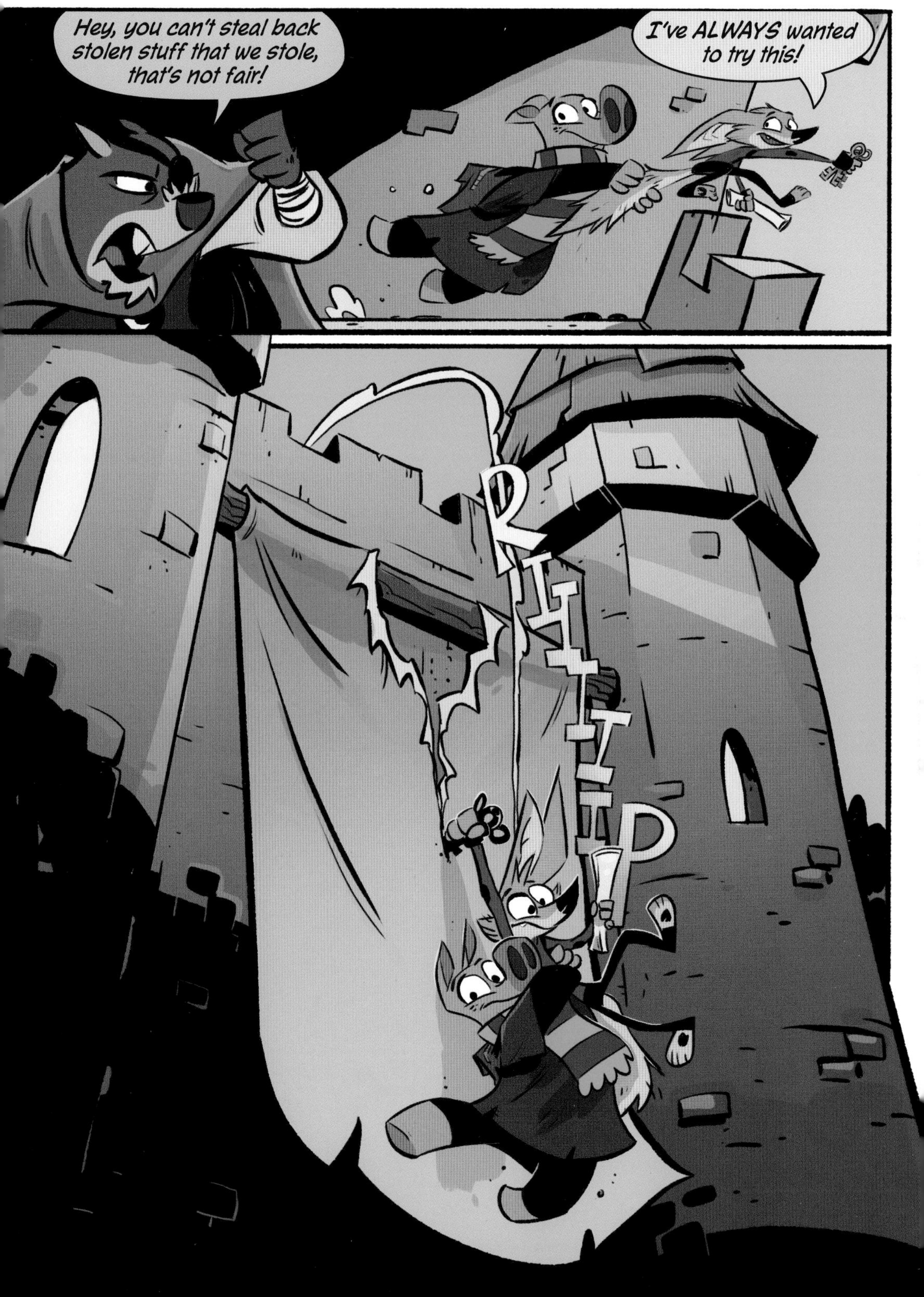
Hey, you can't steal back stolen stuff that we stole, that's not fair!
I've ALWAYS wanted to try this!
RIIIIP

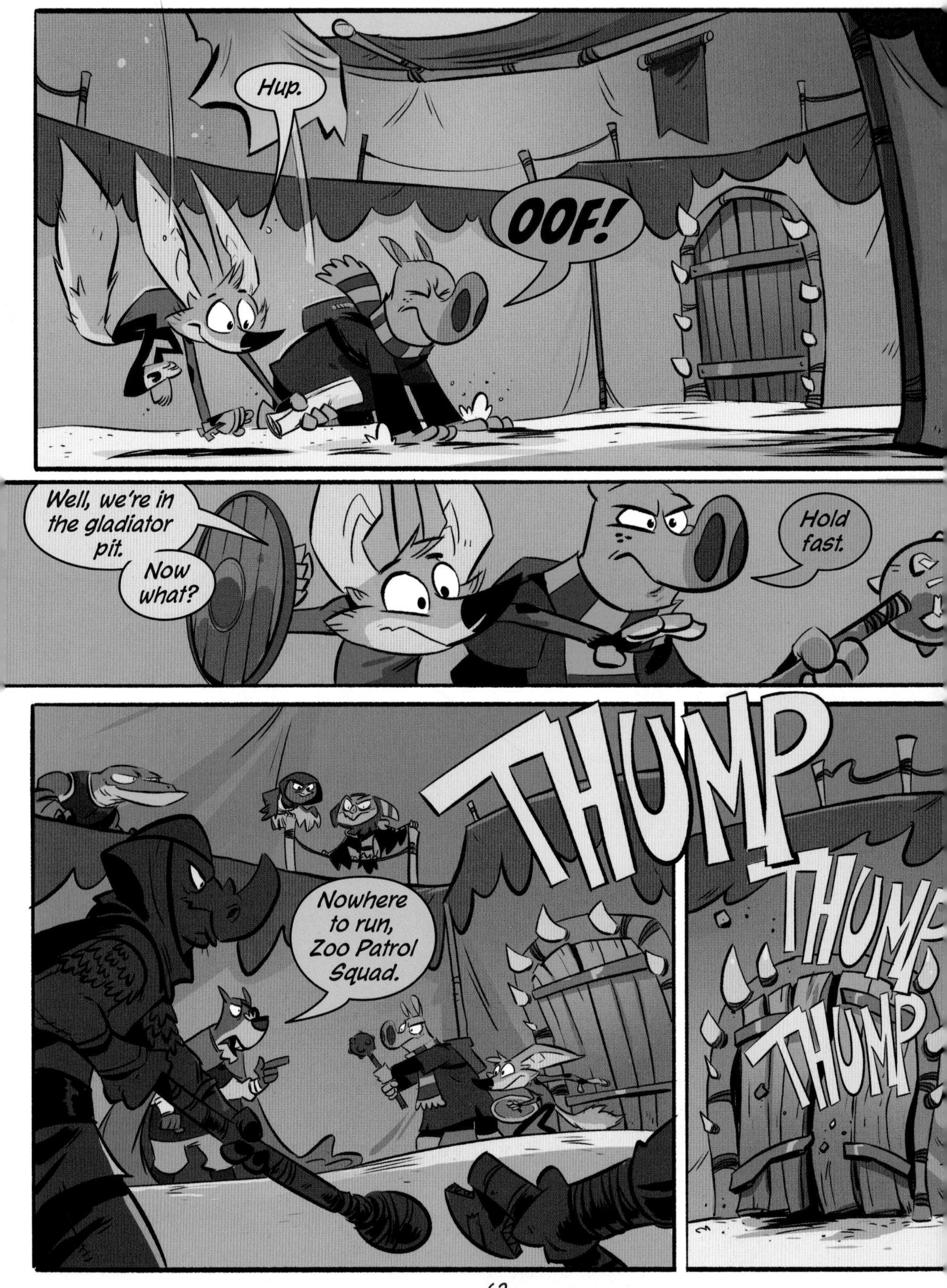
Hup.
OOF!
Well, we're in the gladiator pit.
Now what?
Hold fast.
THUMP
Nowhere to run, Zoo Patrol Squad.
THUMP
THUMP

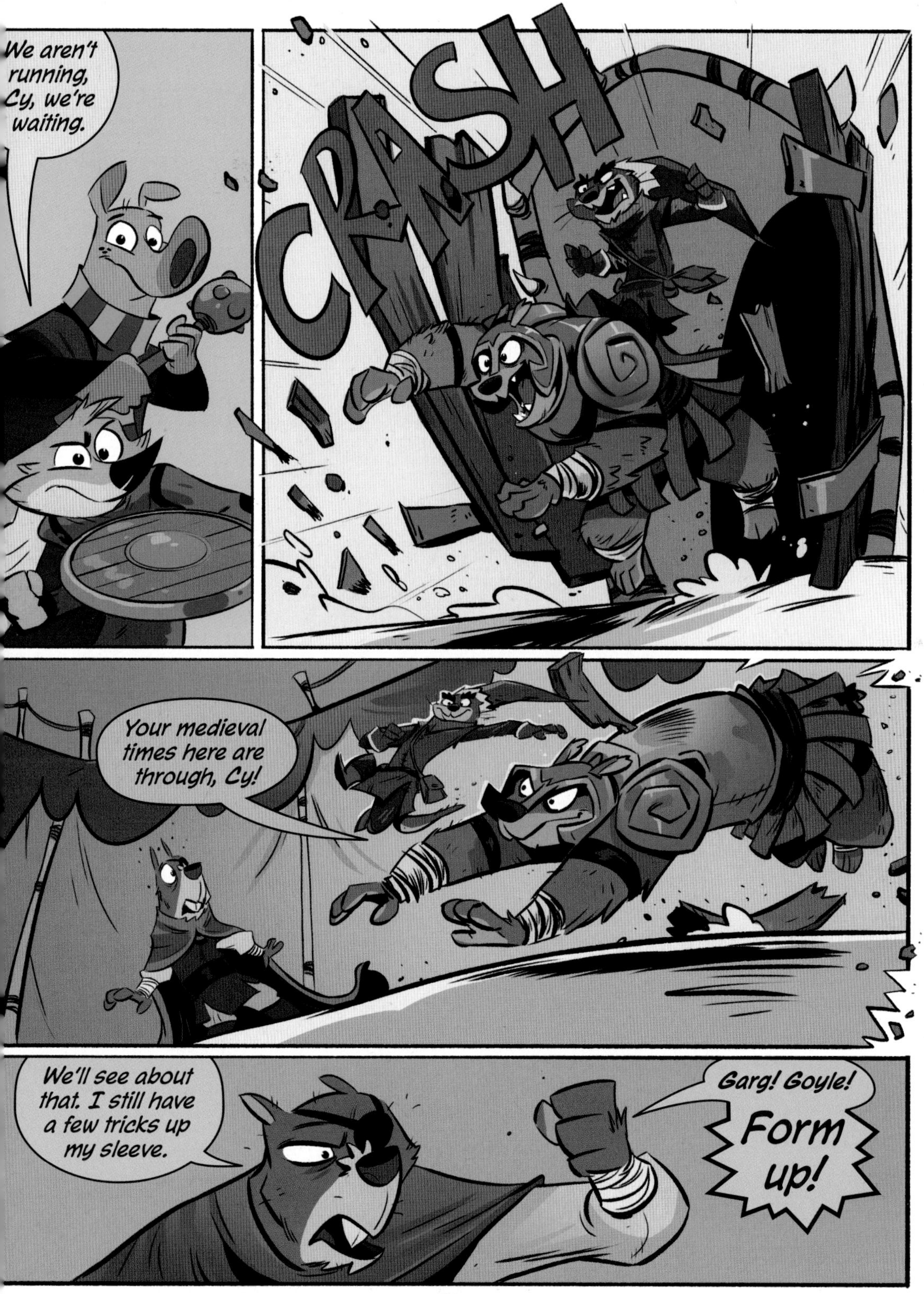
We aren't running, Cy, we're waiting.
CRASH
Your medieval times here are through, Cy!
We'll see about that. I still have a few tricks up my sleeve.
Garg! Goyle!
Form up!

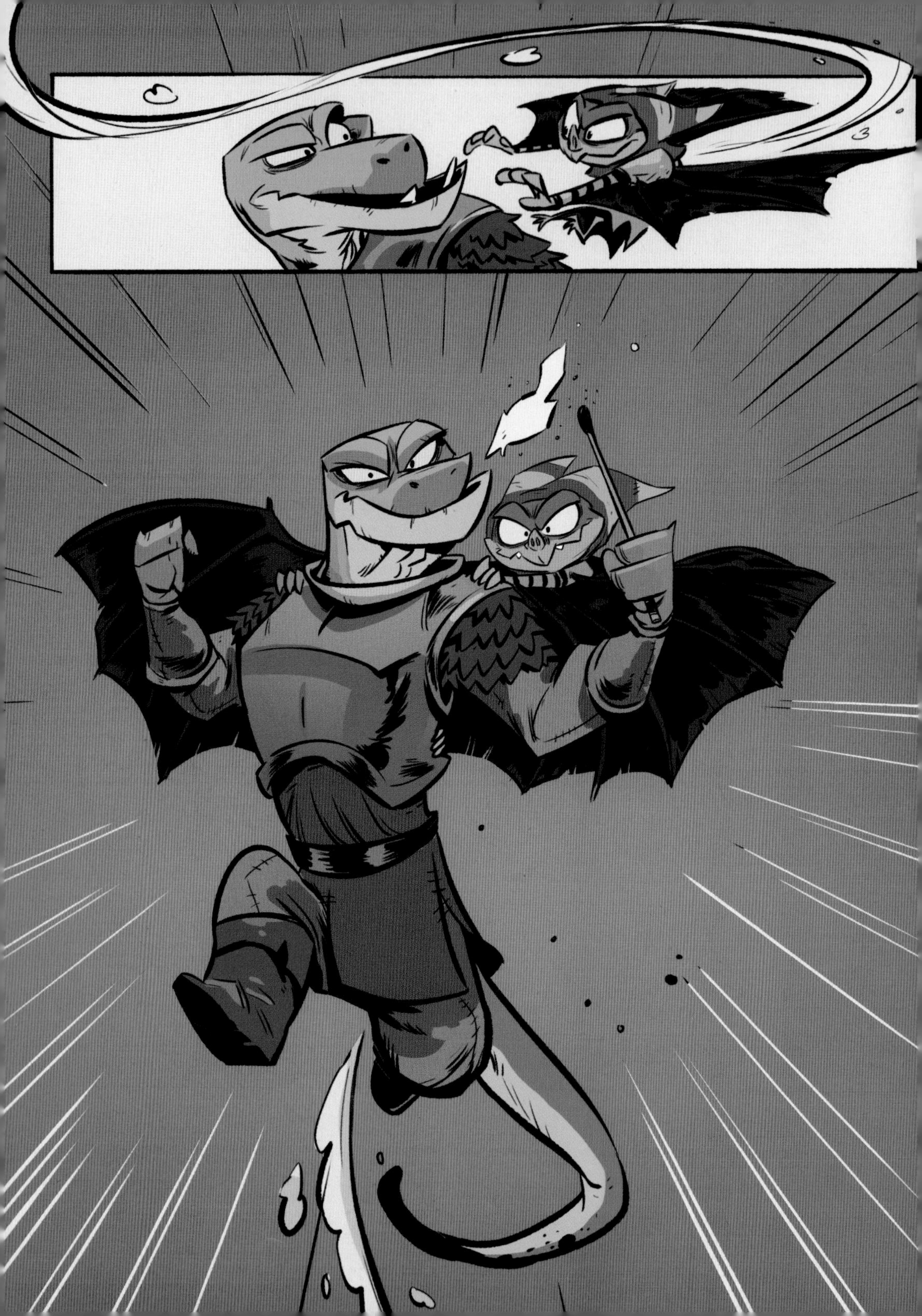

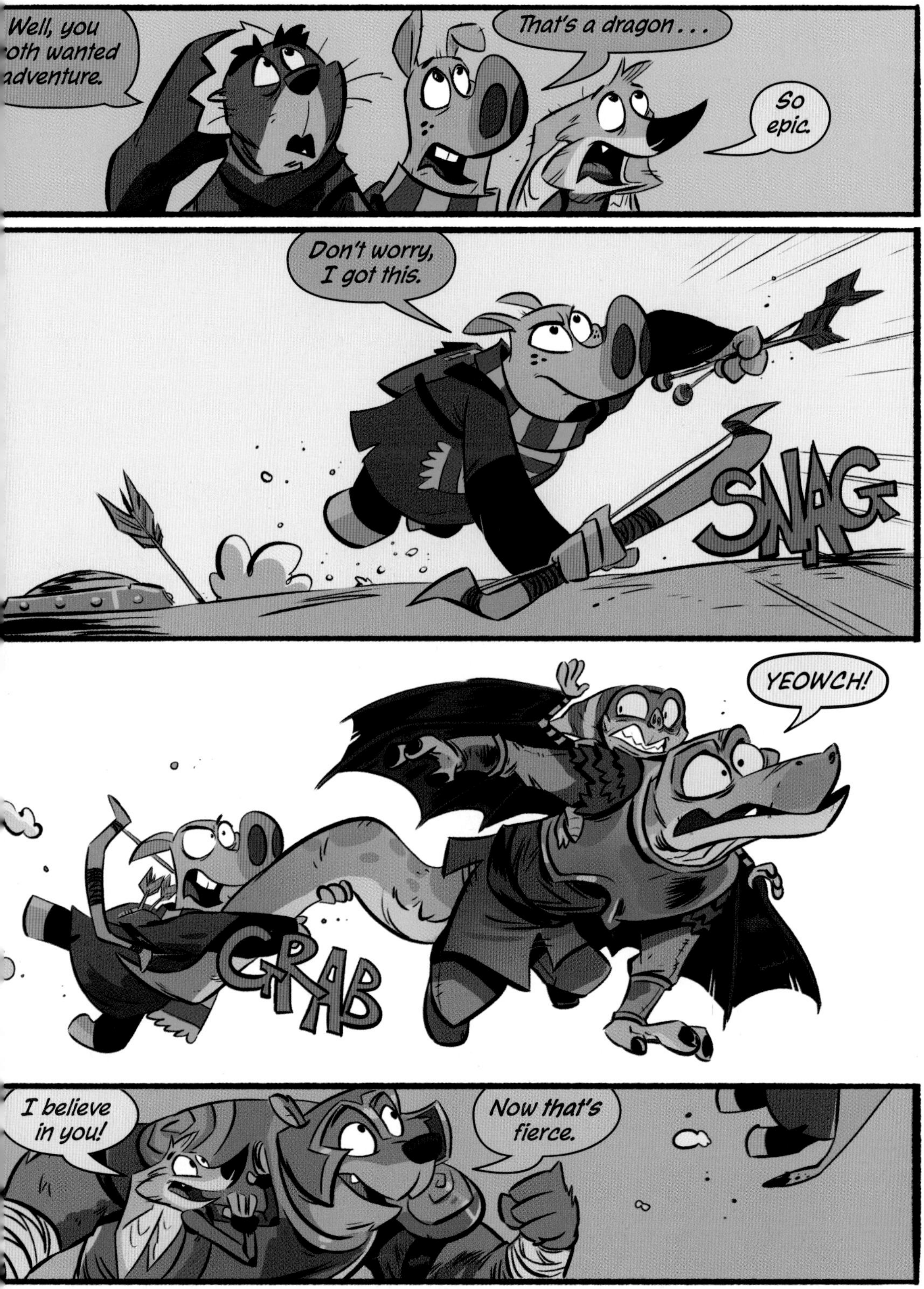
Well, you oth wanted adventure.
That's a dragon . . .
So epic.
Don't worry, I got this.
SNAG
YEOWCH!
GRAB
I believe in you!
Now that's fierce.

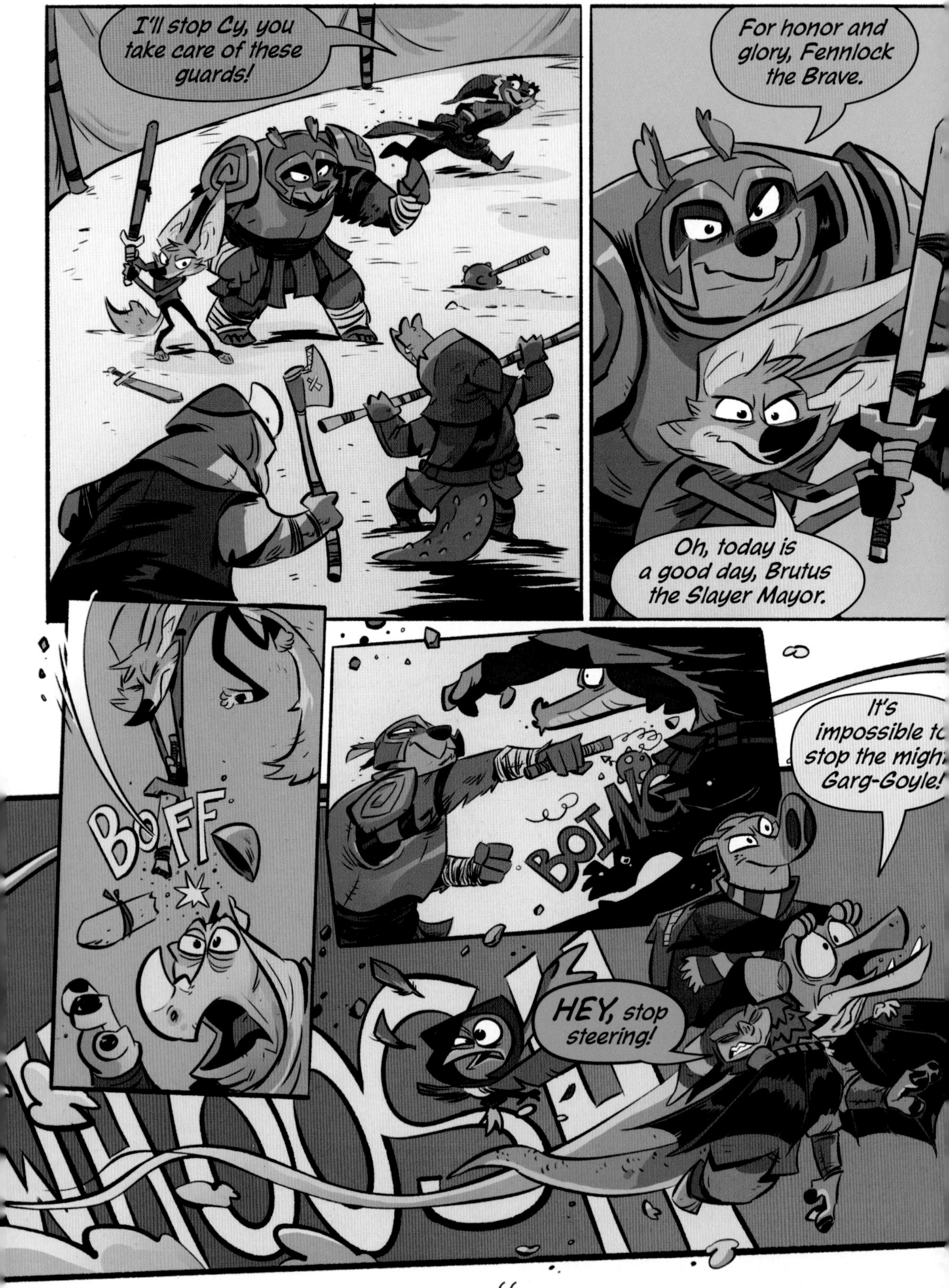

I'll stop Cy, you take care of these guards!
For honor and glory, Fennlock the Brave.
Oh, today is a good day, Brutus the Slayer Mayor.
BOFF
BOING
It's impossible to stop the mighty Garg-Goyle!
HEY, stop steering!

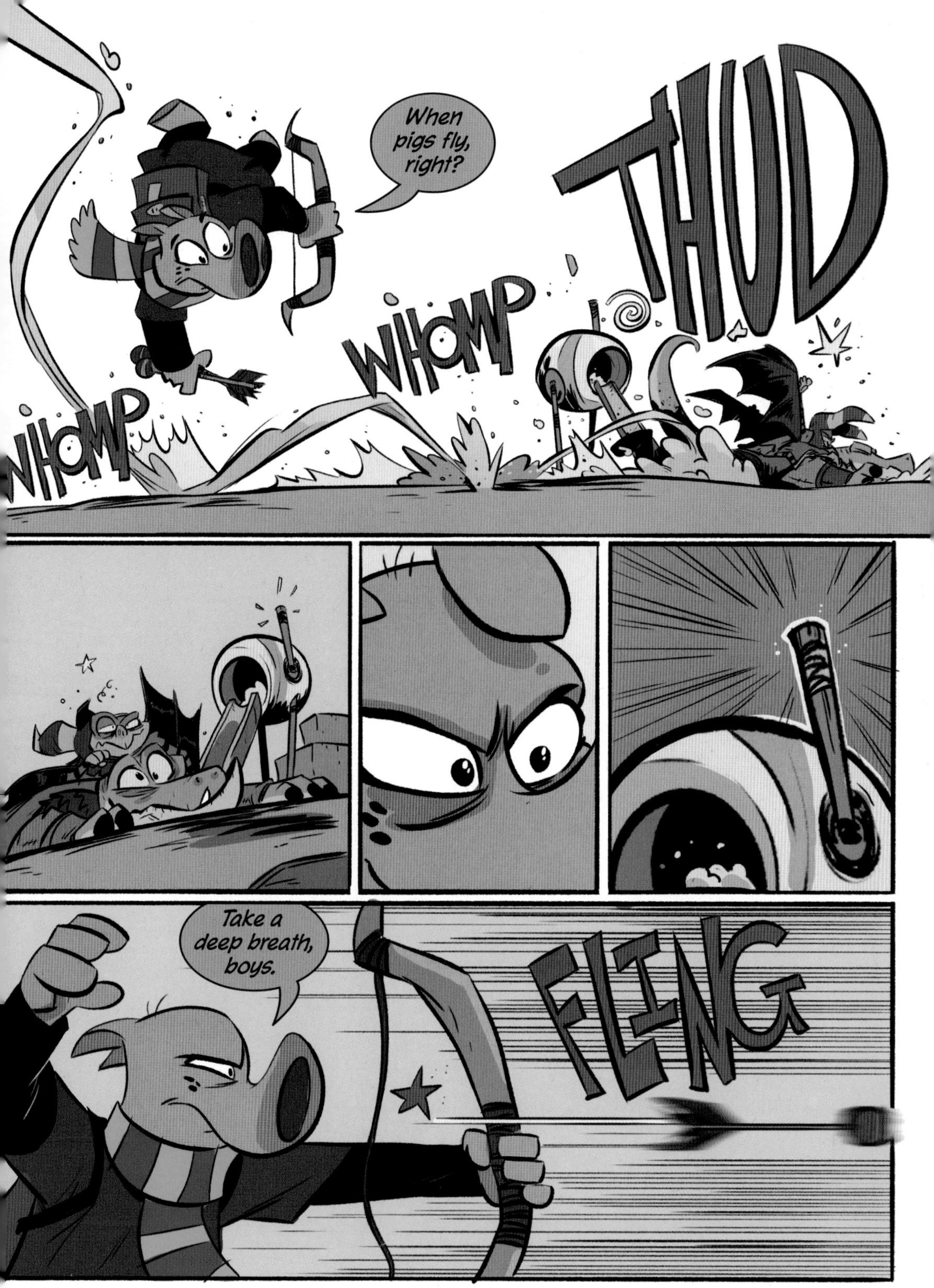
When pigs fly, right?
WHOMP
WHOMP
WHOMP
THUD
Take a deep breath, boys.
FLING

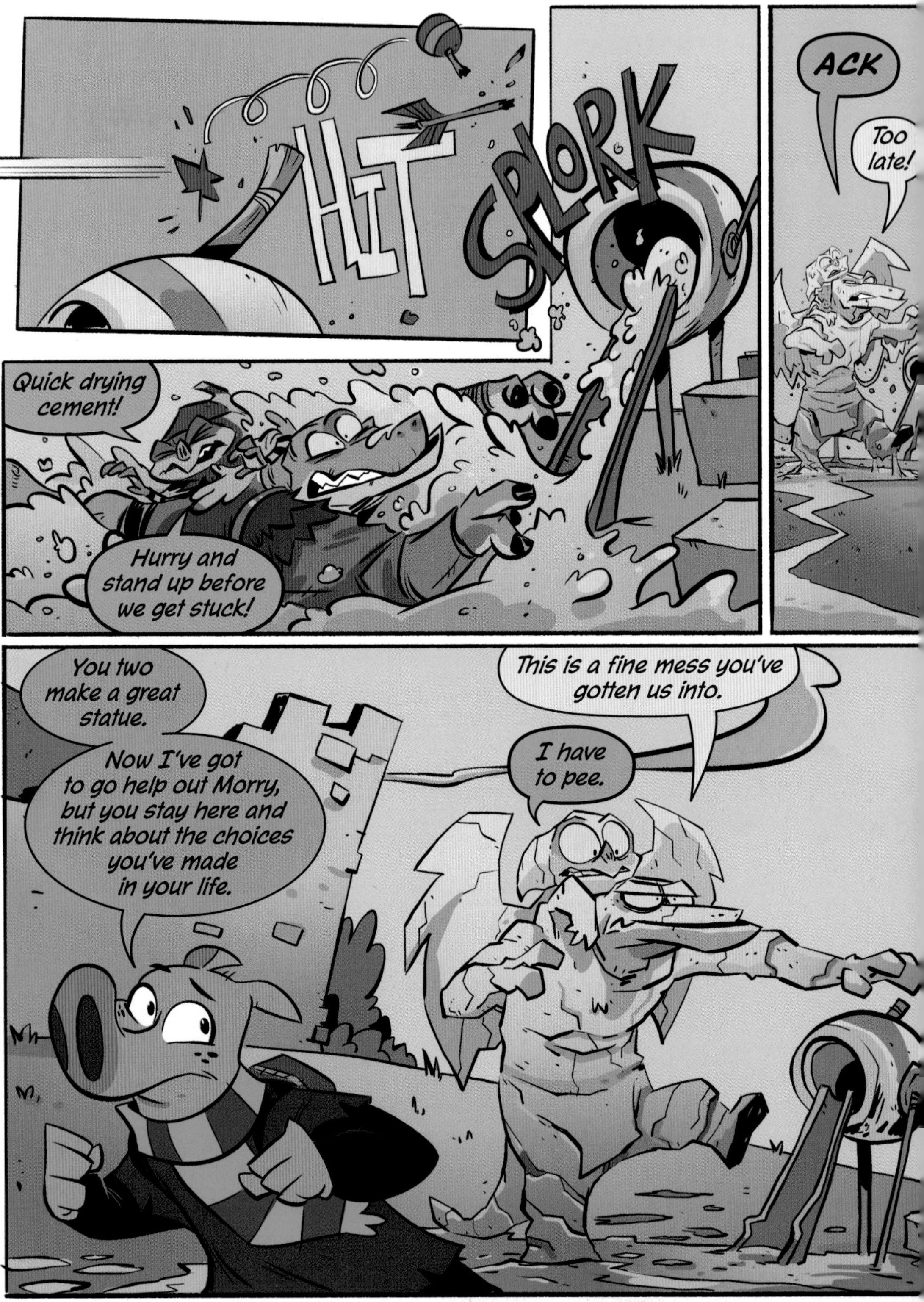
HIT
SPLORK
ACK
Too late!
Quick drying cement!
Hurry and stand up before we get stuck!
You two make a great statue.
Now I've got to go help out Morry, but you stay here and think about the choices you've made in your life.
This is a fine mess you've gotten us into.
I have to pee.

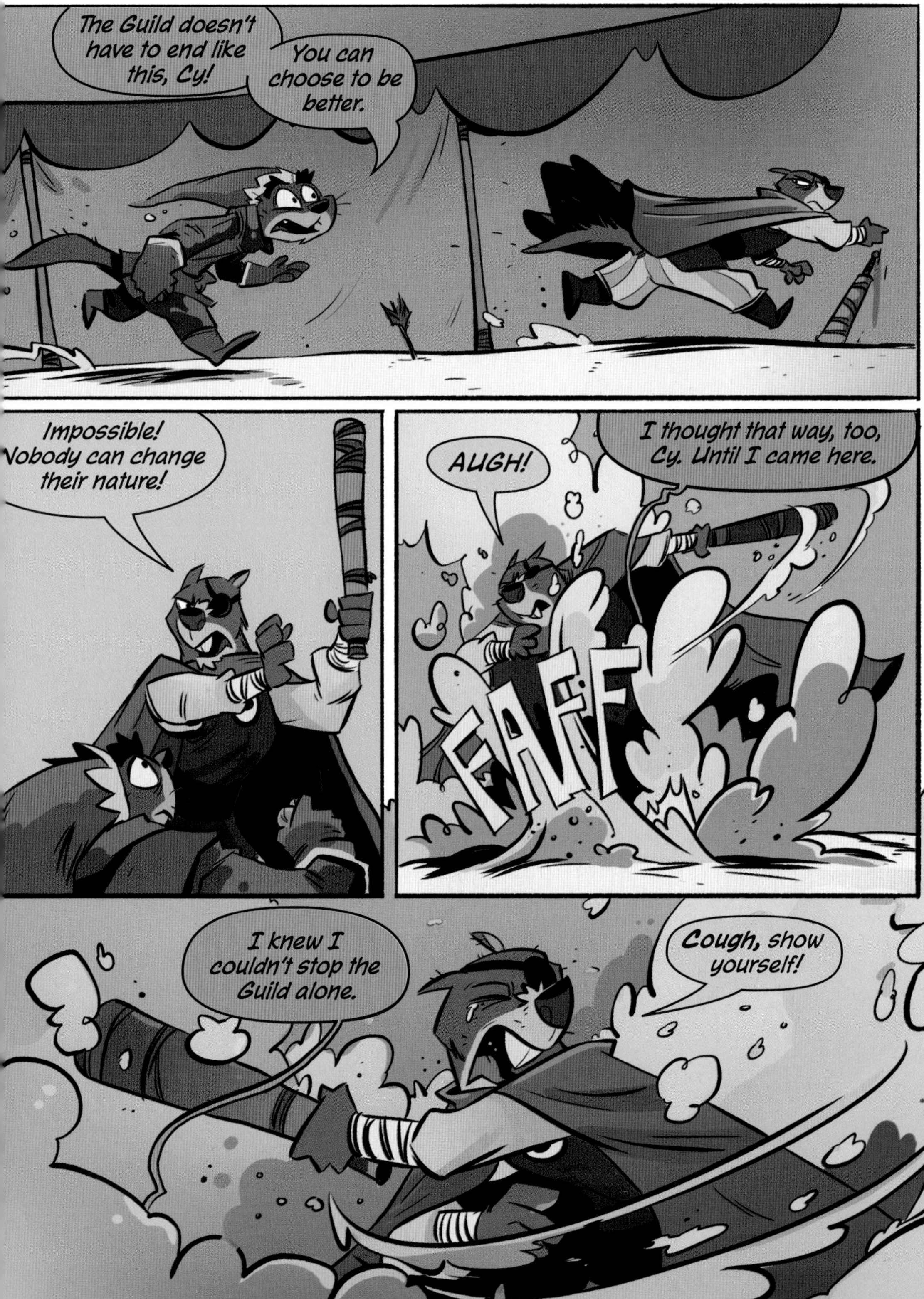

The Guild doesn't have to end like this, Cy!
You can choose to be better.
Impossible! Nobody can change their nature!
AUGH!
I thought that way, too, Cy. Until I came here.
FAFF
I knew I couldn't stop the Guild alone.
Cough, show yourself!

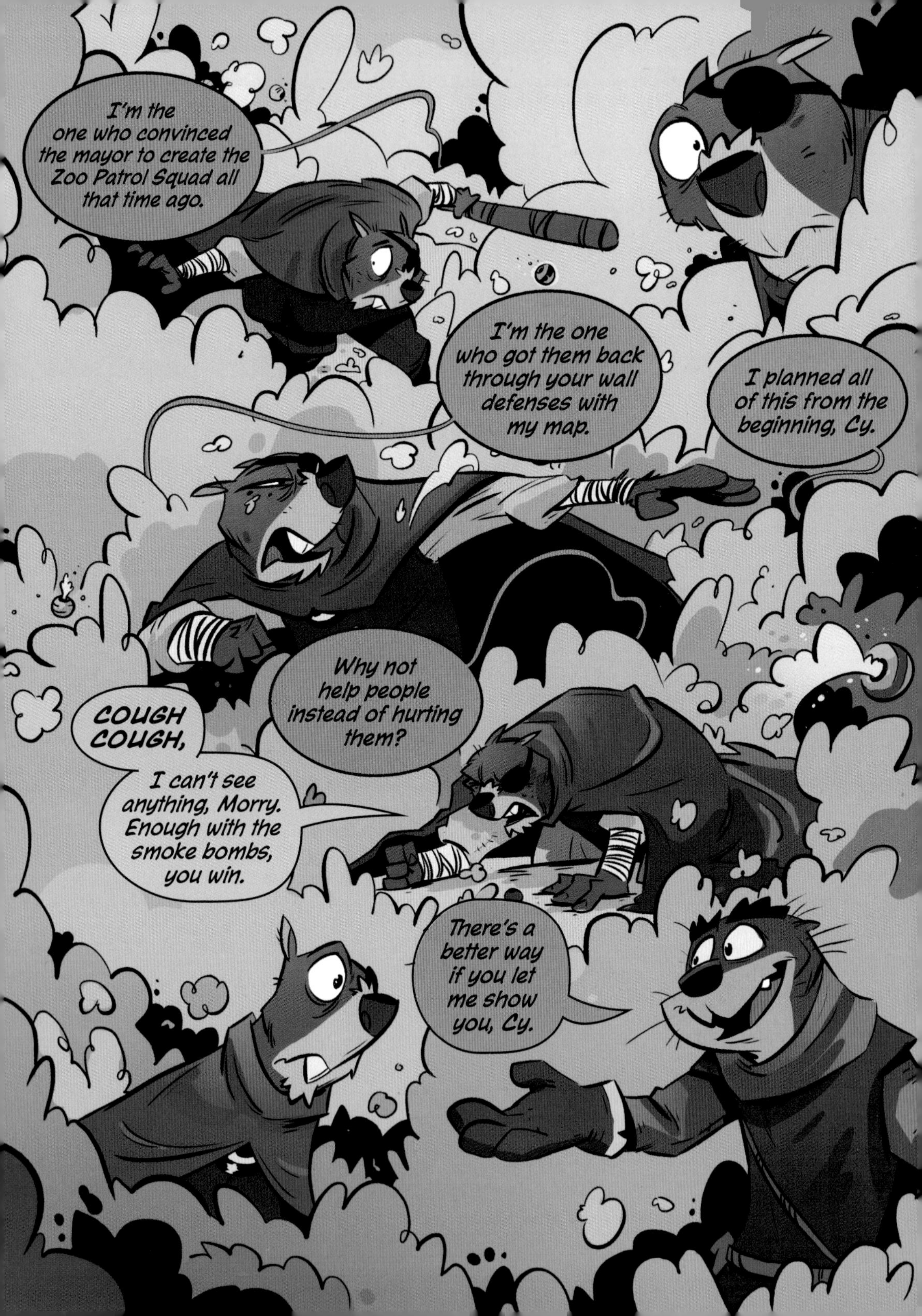
I'm the one who convinced the mayor to create the Zoo Patrol Squad all that time ago.
I'm the one who got them back through your wall defenses with my map.
I planned all of this from the beginning, Cy.
Why not help people instead of hurting them?
COUGH COUGH,
I can't see anything, Morry. Enough with the smoke bombs, you win.
There's a better way if you let me show you, Cy.

I've only taken things without asking, I don't know how to do anything else.

Have you thought about being a private eye?

Very funny.

I'm serious, you and me. We were always a good team back in the day.

If you mean it, I guess we can give it a try.

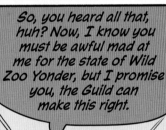

EEP!

So, you heard all that, huh? Now, I know you must be awful mad at me for the state of Wild Zoo Yonder, but I promise you, the Guild can make this right.

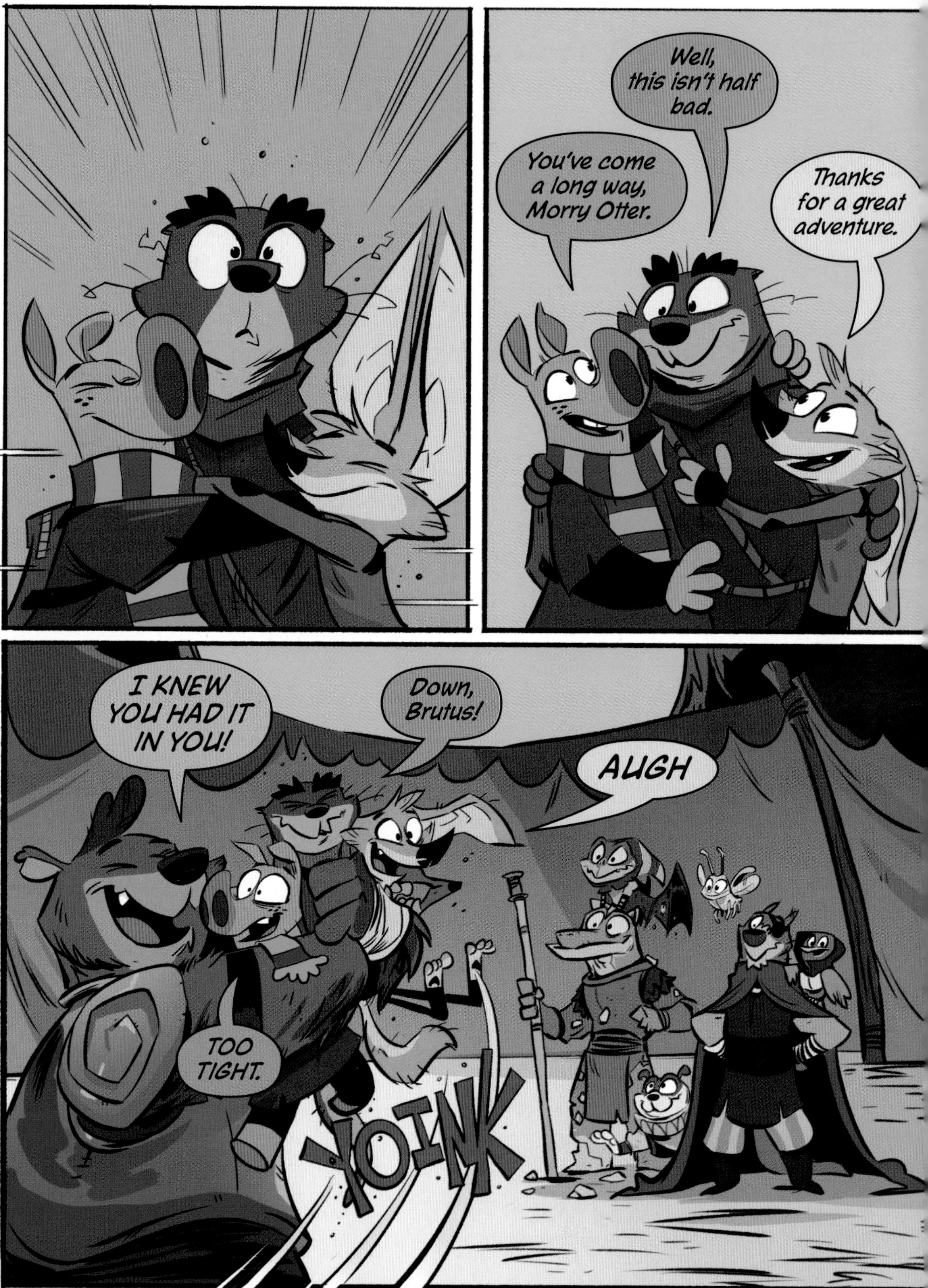

Well, this isn't half bad.
You've come a long way, Morry Otter.
Thanks for a great adventure.
I KNEW YOU HAD IT IN YOU!
Down, Brutus!
AUGH
TOO TIGHT.
YOINK

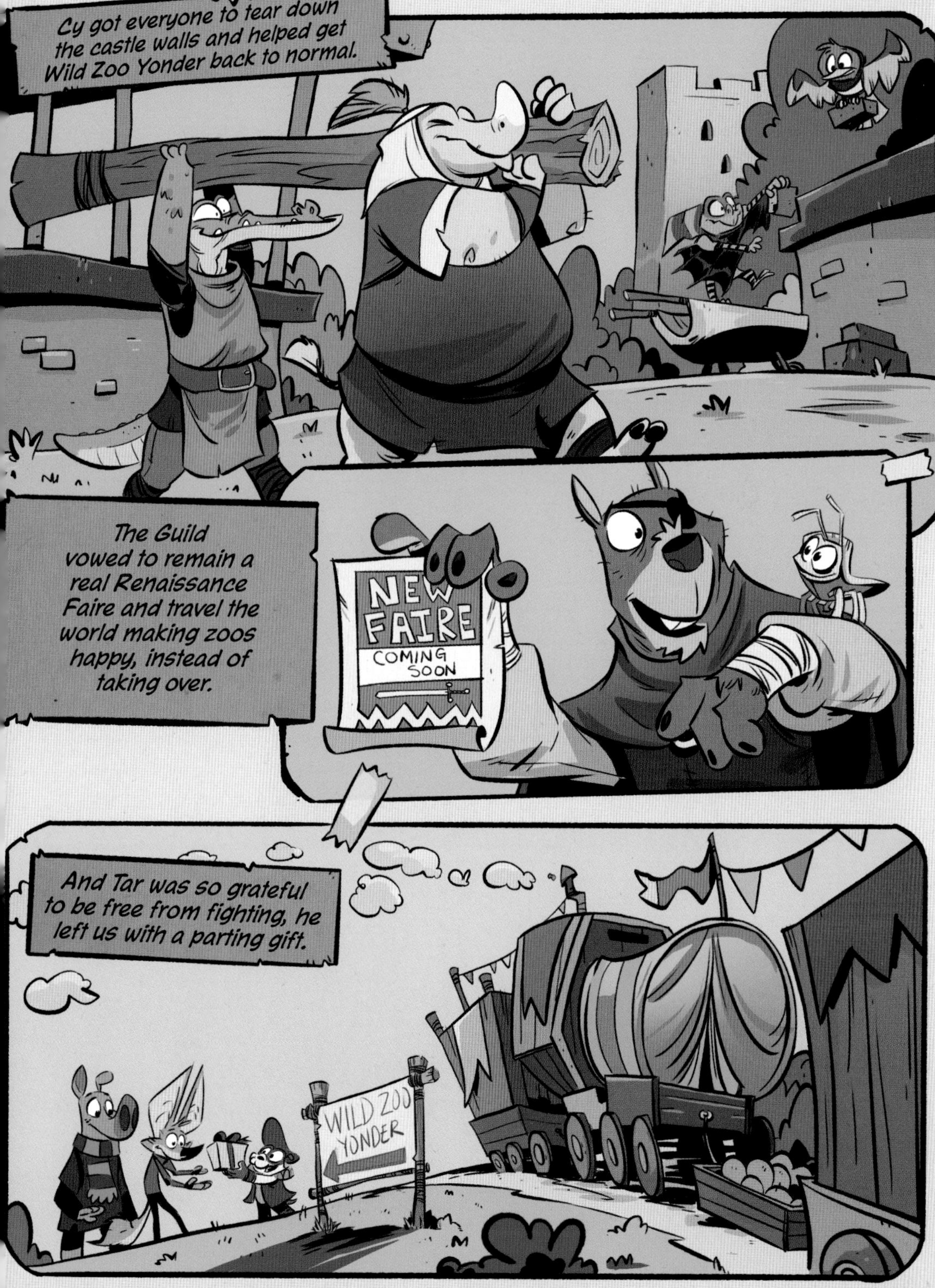
Cy got everyone to tear down the castle walls and helped get Wild Zoo Yonder back to normal.
The Guild vowed to remain a real Renaissance Faire and travel the world making zoos happy, instead of taking over.
NEW FAIRE
COMING SOON
And Tar was so grateful to be free from fighting, he left us with a parting gift.
WILD ZOO YONDER

This fits perfectly.

Tar really knows his craft.

If you two are done admiring yourselves, there is a new assignment ready!

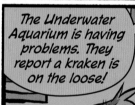

The Underwater Aquarium is having problems. They report a kraken is on the loose!

Sounds like a case for...

MORRY & CY, Private Eye Investigations!

SNAG

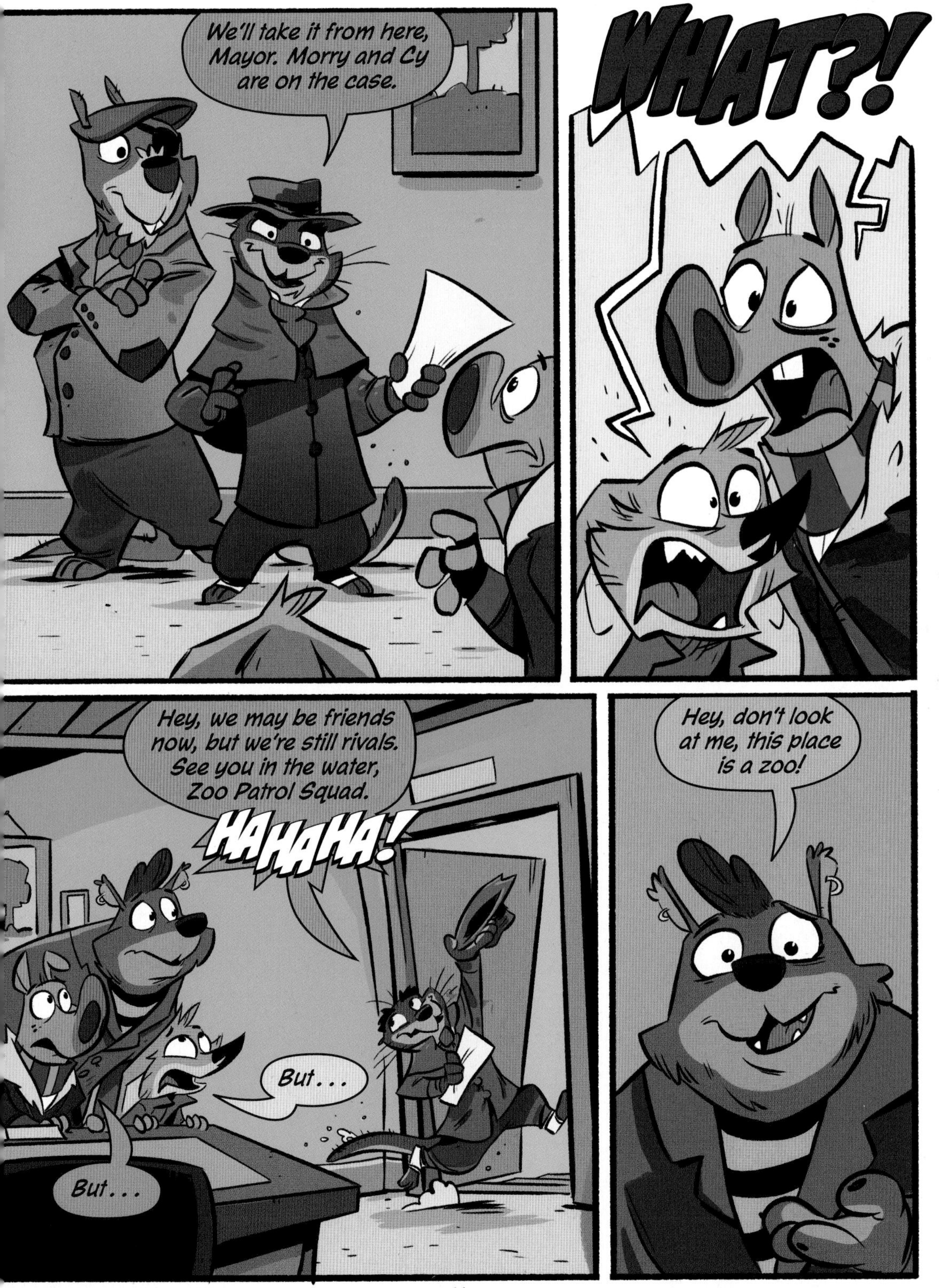
We'll take it from here, Mayor. Morry and Cy are on the case.
WHAT?!
Hey, we may be friends now, but we're still rivals. See you in the water, Zoo Patrol Squad.
HAHAHA!
But...
But...
Hey, don't look at me, this place is a zoo!

PENNY AND FENNLOCK BOOK OF PUZZLES AND FACTS

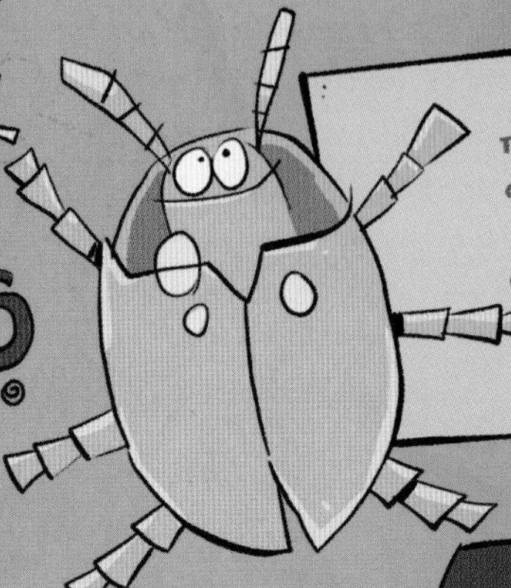

TORTOISE BEETLE

TORTOISE BEETLES ARE OFTEN DARK IN COLOR, BUT MANY HAVE A DISTINCTIVE METALLIC COLORATION, USUALLY GOLD OR ORANGE. THEY CAN ACTUALLY ALTER THEIR METALLIC COLOR TO BLEND IN WITH A LEAF SURFACE.

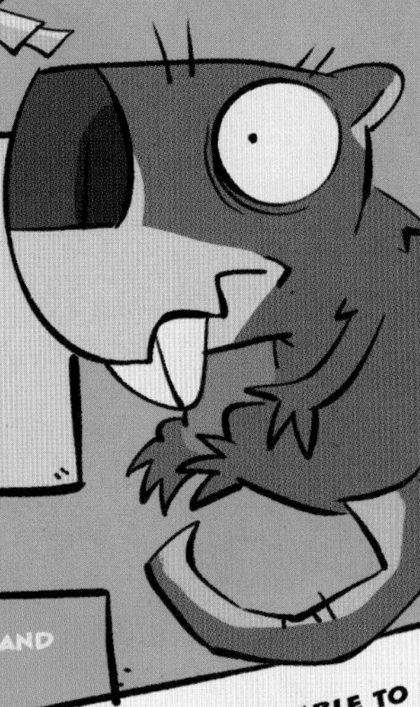

NUTRIA (SWAMP RAT)

ONE OF THE REASONS NUTRIA POSE SUCH A BIG PROBLEM AS AN INVASIVE SPECIES IS THAT THEY MULTIPLY RAPIDLY. THEY CAN REPRODUCE UP TO THREE TIMES A YEAR AND, IN EXTREME CASES, CAN HAVE LITTERS OF UP TO 13!

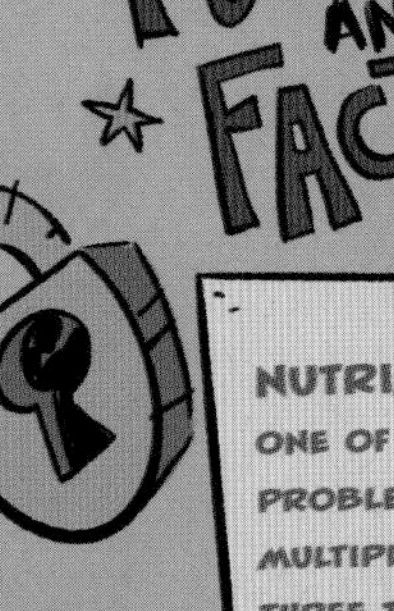

MINIATURE BULL TERRIER

THEY HAVE A HEIGHT OF 10–14 INCHES AND USUALLY WEIGH 25–30 POUNDS.

BATS ARE THE ONLY MAMMALS THAT ARE ABLE TO FLY.

BATS

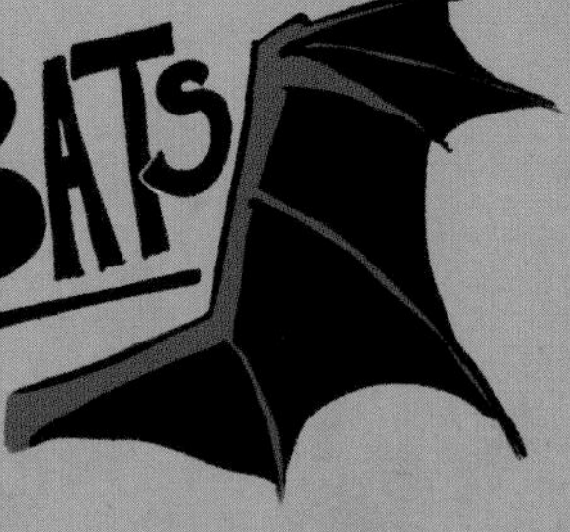

KOMODO DRAGONS ARE THE **LARGEST** LIVING LIZARDS.

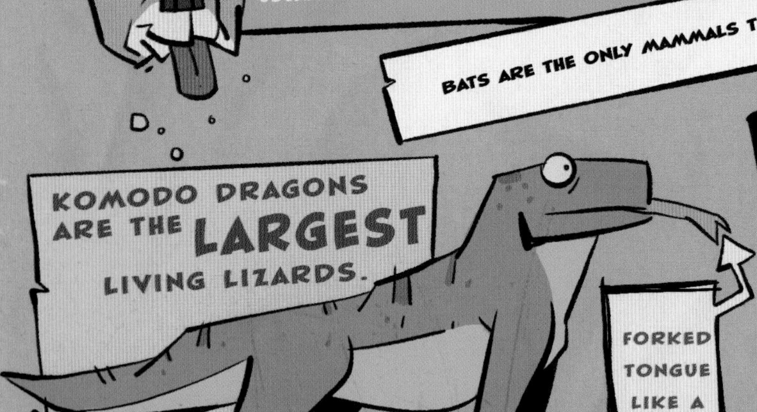

FORKED TONGUE LIKE A SNAKE

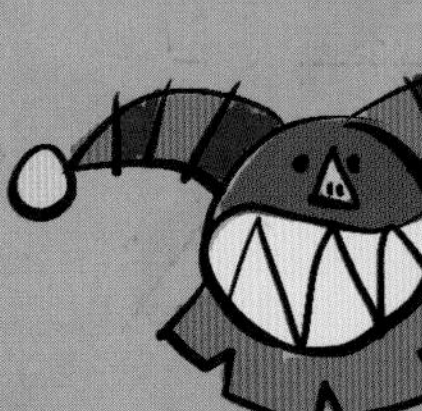

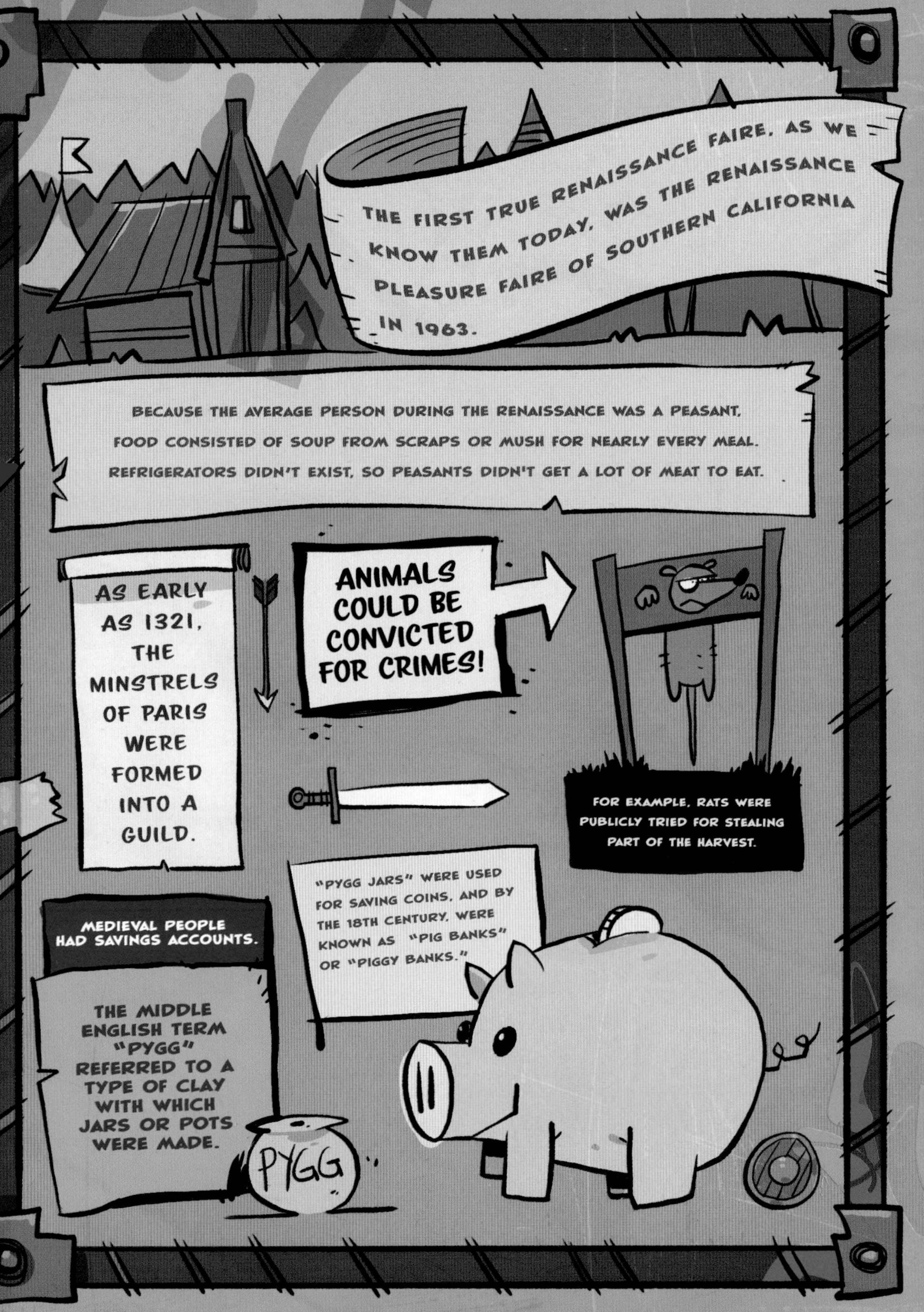
THE FIRST TRUE RENAISSANCE FAIRE, AS WE KNOW THEM TODAY, WAS THE RENAISSANCE PLEASURE FAIRE OF SOUTHERN CALIFORNIA IN 1963.
BECAUSE THE AVERAGE PERSON DURING THE RENAISSANCE WAS A PEASANT, FOOD CONSISTED OF SOUP FROM SCRAPS OR MUSH FOR NEARLY EVERY MEAL. REFRIGERATORS DIDN'T EXIST, SO PEASANTS DIDN'T GET A LOT OF MEAT TO EAT.
AS EARLY AS 1321, THE MINSTRELS OF PARIS WERE FORMED INTO A GUILD.
ANIMALS COULD BE CONVICTED FOR CRIMES!
FOR EXAMPLE, RATS WERE PUBLICLY TRIED FOR STEALING PART OF THE HARVEST.
"PYGG JARS" WERE USED FOR SAVING COINS, AND BY THE 18TH CENTURY, WERE KNOWN AS "PIG BANKS" OR "PIGGY BANKS."
MEDIEVAL PEOPLE HAD SAVINGS ACCOUNTS.
THE MIDDLE ENGLISH TERM "PYGG" REFERRED TO A TYPE OF CLAY WITH WHICH JARS OR POTS WERE MADE.
PYGG

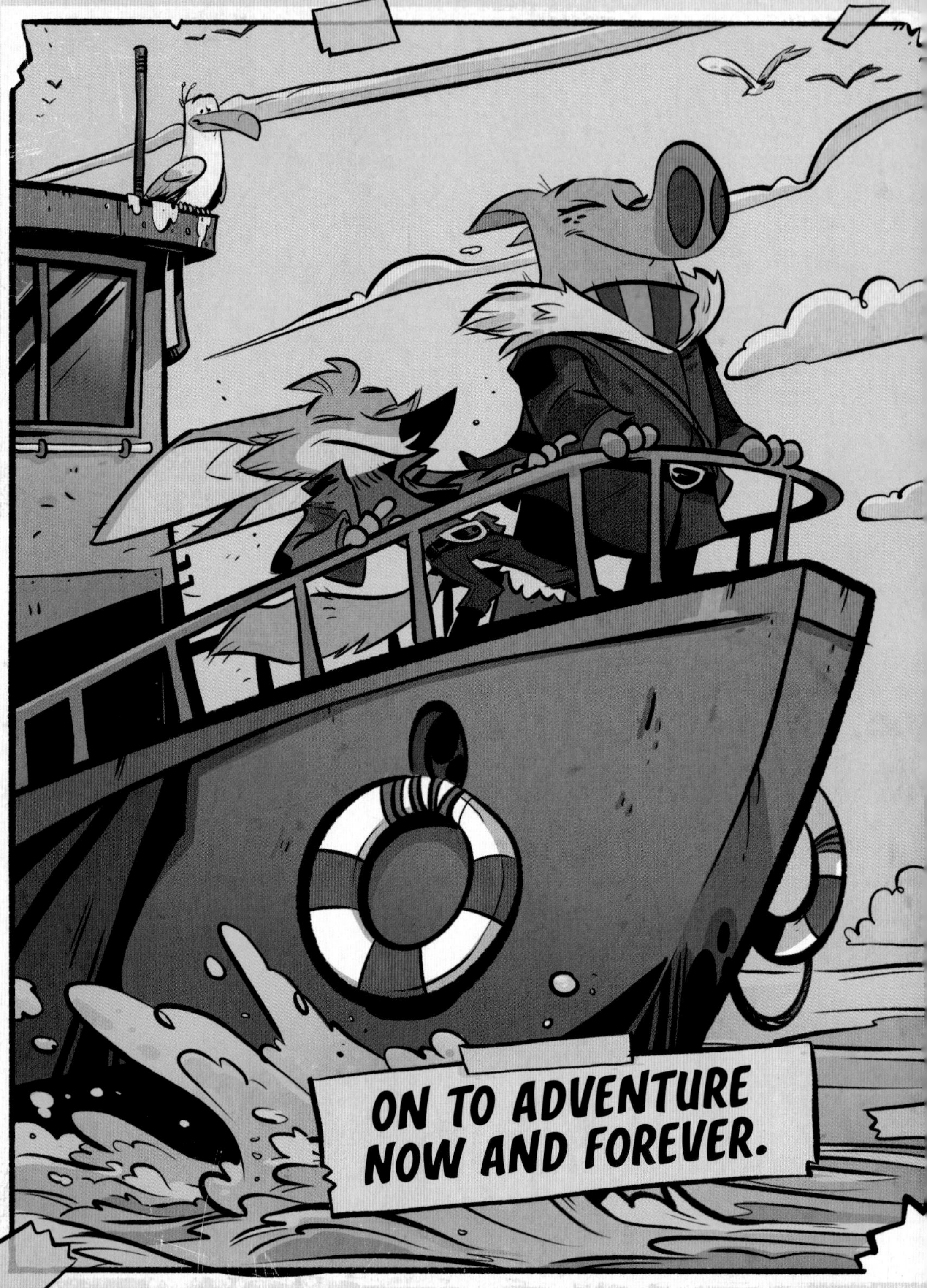
ON TO ADVENTURE
NOW AND FOREVER.